TOUGH DAY FOR THE ARMY

Yellow Shoe Fiction
Michael Griffith, Series Editor

TOUGH DAY
FOR THE ARMY

stories

John Warner

LOUISIANA STATE UNIVERSITY PRESS
BATON ROUGE

Published with the assistance of the Borne Fund

Published by Louisiana State University Press
Copyright © 2014 by Louisiana State University Press
All rights reserved
Manufactured in the United States of America
LSU Press Paperback Original
First printing

DESIGNER: Michelle A. Neustrom
TYPEFACE: Adobe Garamond Pro
PRINTER AND BINDER: Maple Press

LIBRARY OF CONGRESS CATALOGING-IN-PUBLICATION DATA

Warner, John, 1970–
    [Short stories. Selections]
    Tough day for the army : stories / John Warner.
        pages ; cm. — (Yellow shoe fiction)
    ISBN 978-0-8071-5802-9 (pbk. : alk. paper) — ISBN 978-0-8071-5803-6 (pdf) —
ISBN 978-0-8071-5804-3 (epub) — ISBN 978-0-8071-5805-0 (mobi)
    I. Warner, John, 1970– II. Title.
    PS3623.A86328A6 2014
    813'.6—dc23
                                                            2014011185

These stories have appeared previously (sometimes in radically different form) in the following publications: "Return-to-Sensibility Problems after Penetrating Captive Bolt Stunning of Cattle in Commercial Beef Slaughter Plant #5867: Confidential Report," *Ninth Letter;* "Monkey and Man," *Bull: Fiction for Men;* "Corrections and Clarifications" and "My Best Seller," *Swink;* "Second Careers," *The Morning News;* "Homosexuals Threaten the Sanctity of Norman's Marriage," *Pank;* "Notes from a Neighborhood War," *McSweeney's Internet Tendency;* "Tuesday, the Bad Zoo," *Zoetrope All-Story Extra;* "What I Am, What I Found, What I Did," *McNeese Review;* "Poet Farmers," *Chicago Reader;* "Tough Day for the Army," *Tarpaulin Sky, McSweeney's Quarterly;* "A Love Story," *Printers Row Journal.*

The paper in this book meets the guidelines for permanence and durability of the Committee on Production Guidelines for Book Longevity of the Council on Library Resources. ∞

For my teachers: past, present, and future

I really do believe we can be better than we are. I know we can.
But the price is enormous—and people are not yet willing to pay it.
　　　—JAMES BALDWIN

I'm not proud, but I'm not an animal either.
　　　—MARK BROOKSTEIN

CONTENTS

TOUGH DAY FOR THE ARMY

Nelson v. the Mormon Smile

Nelson was worried about his balls, and because Nelson was the kind of person who tended to put his thoughts into words, he leaned over to the cubicle next to him and said to his friend/coworker, Jürgen, "I'm worried about my balls."

Jürgen held up a finger, signaling that Nelson should wait. Jürgen spoke into his headset mouthpiece, asking if Mrs. Luffnagel was home. "Hello? Hello? Mrs. Luffnagel?" He punched the ESC key on his computer and leaned back in his chair to look Nelson in the eye. "Answering machine," he said. Nelson and Jürgen worked as interviewers for Survey Circle, Inc., Marketing Researchers. The computers in front of them were engaged in predictive dialing, calling many numbers at once, trying to find one with a live human on the other end so Nelson and Jürgen and the twenty-five other workers on their shift could ask questions. Tonight the questions were about fast food; how much, how often, what kinds, degrees of satisfaction, when they anticipated visiting next. Nelson sometimes thought about inserting "having intercourse" into the script wherever it said "eating fast food," but he knew that would be juvenile, and besides he needed the job.

Each week fewer and fewer of the numbers seemed to hit, so Jürgen and Nelson had plenty of time to talk.

"Why are you worried about your balls?"

"Radiation," Nelson said. "From cell phones. Turns out they cook your balls if you keep your phone in your pocket. I've been carrying my phone in my pocket every waking hour for the past four years. The rats in this study I read about got 'marble-sized' tumors in less than three months. I can't even look at what's going on down there. I shower with my eyes closed."

"How did the rats keep the phones in their pockets?"

"I dunno. I guess they like taped the phones to their junk."

"Sounds cruel. You know what you should be worried about?"

"What's that?"

"Your deodorant."

"Oh yeah? Why's that?"

"Aluminum chlorohydrate—it gives you Alzheimer's."

"Fuck."

Lance Riggins, one cube over from Jürgen, leaned past the cubicle walls, showing his cinder-block head, face as broad as a cereal box, and glared at Nelson. Nelson flipped him the bird in return and mouthed, "Screw you." Survey Circle, Inc., was owned and operated by Mormons, which made sense because they were located in Provo, Utah. Ninety-five percent of the employees were Mormon, almost all of them students at BYU, which meant nasty looks if you said "Fuck" and no coffee machine in the break room. Nelson and Jürgen got hired because Survey Circle, Inc., needed to keep a certain percentage of non-Mormons on the payroll so the federal government didn't come down on them for discrimination. Nelson and Jürgen had, for all practical purposes, total job security, since there were very few non-Mormons in Provo, and an even smaller percentage of the non-Mormon Provoians had a desire to work for Survey Circle Marketing Research, Inc. A Venn diagram would show a very small intersection, with only Nelson and Jürgen inside.

Nelson and Jürgen were supposed to be in Park City, not Provo, teaching snowboarding to hot college chicks on vacation, but Nelson and Jürgen failed the drug test because they both liked pot, because—what the fuck?—they were snowboarders. They didn't anticipate the piss test, but there's insurance involved and shit, and they took it anyway, certain they would fail on the merits, but hoping for some kind of clerical error in their favor. But now they were "flagged," as in no jobs teaching snowboarding in the state of Utah, period. The work they could get was at Survey Circle, Inc., which didn't have a drug-testing policy because Mormons don't do drugs because if they did they wouldn't have any space reserved for them in the celestial kingdom, which Nelson understood to be a kind of endless family reunion lit up by the very bright light of God.

Nelson had no truck with the Mormon view of the afterlife. He had zero interest in meeting up with most of his relatives for an afternoon, let alone eternity, except his mother, who died when Norman was three, so it's not like they'd even recognize each other anyway, unless in the celestial kingdom everyone has name tags, or somehow just knows who is who. Norman left home just under a year after his father had sneered at the long hair coming out from under his ski cap and said he looked like a "faggot." Jürgen came with because why not? Sure, Jürgen had been accepted to Dartmouth, but Dartmouth was older even than the United States of America and wasn't going anywhere, and the chance to move three-quarters of the way across the country with your best and oldest friend to teach hot chicks snowboarding presented itself exactly once.

Vermont was good for snowboarding, but bad for Nelson because it was filled with people who did not understand him, most specifically his father, who knew Nelson wasn't a "faggot" because Nelson's father had walked in on him having sex with Nelson's father's (presumably now ex-) girlfriend. Nelson's father had been understandably upset on that occasion, but while it was the two of them (Nelson and Christine) doing the horizontal mambo, it was Nelson alone who got his ass kicked because his pops was an honorable man who wouldn't hit a broad.

Nelson wasn't in love with Christine, but he thought he might be in love with Chelsea Stubbins, who happened to be Lance Riggins's girlfriend, and also happened to work at Survey Circle, Inc. Nelson understood that one of the reasons he smoked a lot of grass was that he liked to get high, and that another one of the reasons he smoked a lot of grass was because he possessed a barely suppressed rage that only a nice indica/sativa blend could tamp down to manageable levels.

The rage, Nelson was sure, was thanks to his father, who used Old Crow as his own suppressor of choice, but Old Crow only worked when he'd drunk so much that he passed out. Up to that point, the alcohol seemed to be a rage amplifier. Mostly his father raged at things on the television, but every so often, Nelson got caught in the crosshairs.

Leaving helped.

Except that he found himself thwarted in his desire to date and make love to Chelsea Stubbins by the likes of Lance Riggins, whose very blond perfection kindled Nelson's rage. Lance Riggins had a jaw, prominent, and abdominal muscles, also prominent, as illustrated by his offer to let anyone who wished to punch him in the stomach. Chelsea Stubbins had the face, beautiful, and the tits and ass, incredible. Also the Mormonism, which meant nobody save her husband was going to be making love to Chelsea Stubbins, particularly not Lance Riggins since that was a double Mormon whammy. It's not like Nelson was eager for Chelsea Stubbins and Lance Riggins to have sex, but for Chelsea Stubbins not to be having sex really was a shame, like owning a Ferrari but keeping it in the garage, which was the kind of dumbass thing Nelson's old man would say, which didn't make it wrong.

Nelson saw Chelsea Stubbins and Lance Riggins get up from their adjoining cubicles and head for the break room. Lance Riggins bumped his shoulder into Chelsea Stubbins, sending her briefly off stride, and she laughed and skipped to catch back up with Lance Riggins. Nelson watched this and felt the rage boil in his fists. He pulled a sheet of scratch paper from the printer on his desk and started drawing on it with a marker.

"What's up?" Jürgen said, peering past his cubicle wall.

"We're having a party."

"Cool, when?"

"Tomorrow."

"Nice. Who's coming?"

"Chelsea Stubbins and Lance Riggins and anyone else who wants to."

Jürgen raised his eyebrows and whistled but didn't say anything else as Nelson finished with the paper and marker and went to the break room where he slapped the notice on the refrigerator using one of the many smiley-face magnets affixed to the surface. Lance Riggins and Chelsea Stubbins sat at a small circular table, sharing a Splenda-sweetened Sprite, Chelsea Stubbins's hands wrapped around the can, Lance Riggins's hands wrapped around Chelsea Stubbins's hands.

"We're having a party," Nelson said, waving at his flyer. On it he'd drawn a crude heart with the initials *LR* + *CS* inside, plus the party information: time, place, hosts.

"What's the occasion?" Lance Riggins replied, releasing Chelsea Stubbins's hands and kicking back in his chair.

"For you, and her," Nelson said, jerking his thumb at Chelsea Stubbins. For some reason he didn't want to say Chelsea's name. "You're the best couple ever, and me and Jürgen thought we should celebrate your example to the rest of us."

Chelsea Stubbins's face pulled in on itself, and she went, "Awwww," in a manner so perfectly sincere that to Nelson it seemed insincere, but he knew that Chelsea Stubbins was incapable of insincerity. Lance Riggins, on the other hand, was well acquainted with Nelson's hostility, with the kicks to the back of his chair as Nelson walked by, with the middle finger salute for no good reason, and so he might've been rightfully suspicious of Nelson's motives, but Lance Riggins was also extremely confident, had life by the short hairs, as Nelson's old man would say (though Lance Riggins would never be so crude), so he didn't particularly give a poop if Nelson was mocking him. The Nelsons of the world were flies off the backs of the Lance Rigginses. Lance Riggins smiled at Nelson. He always smiled at Nelson, and everyone else for that matter. That smile made no sense to Nelson, where it might come from, what it was rooted to. Nelson thought he might be able to boot Lance Riggins in the balls and he'd still smile about it.

"Wouldn't miss it," Lance Riggins said. He shot forward in his chair, grabbed the can out of Chelsea Stubbins's grip, and drank the rest of it in two large swallows, his Adam's apple bobbing manfully up and down. Finished, he crushed the can in his fist and lobbed it for the recycling bin, turning his back with the can still midflight. The can glanced off the rim and skidded across the floor toward Nelson's feet.

Chelsea Stubbins yelled "Hey," to Lance Riggins's retreating form, but he never broke stride on his way back to his cubicle. Nelson stared down at the can as Chelsea Stubbins plucked it from the ground and tossed it into the bin in a flawless motion.

"Nice shot," Nelson said, and Chelsea Stubbins smiled at him and Nelson felt like he'd been tasered.

That all happened on Friday, so on Saturday, the day of the party, Nelson spent his time on two things.

One was looking in the mirror and willing his face to change into some different, more Lance Riggins–esque shape. He was fresh out of the shower, enjoying how the Utah air dried him all by itself. The acne had cleared up, at least, but he could still see purple ghosts of the worst eruptions. His father had named one that cropped up on his forehead junior year. "Here comes Vesuvius," he'd say. "And look, it brought Nelson with him," and then he'd laugh like he was the fucking funniest dickhead on the planet.

Nineteen years old and Nelson still didn't need to shave, save a couple of long boys that cropped out of his neck, but despite his boyish face, he felt as though he had the capacity for love of someone much older and wiser, and that love was for Chelsea Stubbins. He flexed his chest muscles in the mirror. Not terrible, physical condition–wise, and he was a hell of a snowboarder, but he was no Lance Riggins in the overall-human-being category. Judging from the stock he came from, he never would be.

Nelson looked down at his deodorant, the ingredient list, and damn if Jürgen wasn't right, "Aluminum Zirconium Tetrachlorohydrex." Jürgen was smart and also trustworthy about these things, so Nelson sniffed his pits, which at least for the moment smelled good from the vanilla-scented bodywash, and tossed the deodorant in the garbage. He pulled his favorite hoodie over his head and stuffed his phone in his sock. They were doing amazing things with prosthetic limbs, but as of yet the balls were irreplaceable, and he wasn't going to live without his phone.

One thing Nelson did not spend his time doing was reading up on Mormonism, because he'd already done that a couple weeks earlier to see if it was something he could get on board with for the sake of Chelsea Stubbins, but that was a definitive no-go. Nelson considered himself spiritual, and though he had some general suspicions about God/religion of the organized variety, he wasn't quite ready to go full atheist. But this Mormon business was such transparent bullshit, a bridge he could not cross, even for Chelsea Stubbins. This Joseph Smith character reminded Nelson of one of his and Jürgen's buddies from back home, Stinkfinger, who did not care for the pot but loved the mushrooms, and when he was peaking could be very convincing about seeing shit like his past lives or the true color of Nelson's aura, or the twin that Bobby Longkiss had eaten in the womb, living inside Bobby's body. Once or twice Stinkfinger gave Nelson the shivers with that shit, but afterwards, with a clearer head, Nelson looked at the guy who got his nickname because he claimed he was the first in school to get to third base and walked around telling everyone to sniff his finger. It was Jürgen who called him out, declaring that Stinkfinger (who had been Daniel up to that moment) had just rubbed his finger around the inside of a tuna can, and Nelson went and retrieved just-about-to-become-Stinkfinger's brown lunch bag out of the trash and brandished the evidence above his head for all to see, and that was that. Stinkfinger was then, and forever, full of shit.

Like this Joseph Smith with his visions, a direct pipeline from God, messages coming direct, like through one of those pneumatic tubes at the bank drive-thru, one of which just happened to be a thumbs-up on plural marriage, because how awesome that God wants you to bang multiple broads who are also totally subservient in the sack and otherwise? Now, Nelson had grown up in Vermont, where there were plenty of liberals, his father being one of the few exceptions. Nelson had been conditioned not to mind if a chick didn't shave her legs, or even her pits, and as far back as middle school, he'd learned about the patriarchal hegemony, the cultural reign of the phallocracy, and could sniff out white male privilege when he saw it.

It bothered him to think that Chelsea Stubbins bought into this horseshit, but Nelson figured it was rooted in the cloistered life—born, raised, surrounded by Mormons. We are who we are with, he figured. He was an exception, he was sure, nothing like his father, the close-minded, reactionary, abusive asshole, but for the most part environment rules, nurture over nature. Once Nelson was able to remove Chelsea Stubbins from the atmosphere of Provo, which was indeed his plan, the Mormonism would fade, like a tan starved of sun.

The other thing Nelson did in preparation for the party was bake. Chocolate brownies with walnuts. Peanut butter cookies with deep fudge swirls and brickle. Rice Krispie treats. All laced with hash. Lots and lots of hash. Nelson had spent the better part of his most recent Survey Circle, Inc., paycheck on hash, which can be acquired anywhere, including Provo, Utah. Jürgen sat in the living room rooting against BYU basketball, occasionally asking if Nelson was sure he wanted to do that.

"Why wouldn't I?"

"Because these kids don't do drugs like we do drugs. They don't do drugs at all."

"That's the point."

"I don't follow."

Nelson removed the latest batch from the oven and began flipping the cookies to the counter for cooling. "It's time for them to snap out of it, to have their minds altered, to realize that things are not always as they seem."

"That's probably illegal," Jürgen replied.

"If truth is a crime, then lock me up," Nelson said.

There'd been a plan, but then things stopped going according to it. The first thing that went wrong was the number of people who showed up. The Survey Circle, Inc., work crew came in bunches and drank Nelson and Jürgen's uncaffeinated soda and ate their salty snacks and even danced in the middle of the small living room to Jürgen's iPod mix of house music. Eventually the salty snacks ran out, and someone went looking through the cupboards and found Nelson's stash of psychotropic baked goods and promptly dug in.

The second thing that went wrong is that seeing this, Nelson had an immediate attack of conscience about these nice people who had been speaking to him in friendly fashions and enjoying Jürgen's music being dosed by him and his hash-laced brownies/cookies/Krispies. However, he knew he could not tell these nice people that the delicious treats were "special," because then when Chelsea Stubbins arrived, they would warn her and she would not partake, so thinking quickly but probably foolishly, he made a joke out of grabbing the brownie/cookie/Krispie out of each individual's hand, shouting, "Cookie monster!" and then shoving them in his own mouth. This got a lot of laughs, and some people started taking a brownie/cookie/Krispie just to see Nelson do it again.

I am taking a tremendous amount of drugs, Nelson thought while he was doing this, which would spur him to the bathroom to purge, after which he would come out only to find that even more people were eating the treats, rinse and repeat, until one of the times he came out of the bathroom and found himself face to face with Jürgen, who gripped him by both shoulders and said, "You are tripping balls, my friend."

"I am tripping balls," Nelson replied, nodding. Jürgen pinched Nelson's wrist between this thumb and two forefingers, counting his pulse. He tilted Nelson's head back to grab the light and looked closely into each pupil one at a time.

"You're OK," Jürgen said. "But no more."

Nelson nodded.

"This is," Jürgen said, jerking his thumb over his shoulder at the increasingly strange scene behind him, "what it will be."

Nelson nodded again, and tears filled his eyes. He hugged Jürgen and wept into his best friend's shoulder. "I love you so much, man."

Jürgen squeezed back. "Love you too, dude. Now, I gotta go do something about this."

Nelson watched Jürgen go back into the living room, where he turned off the music and in his best cruise director voice asked, "Who wants to watch a movie?" To which just about everyone, at least those that weren't already completely engrossed in studying the lines on the backs of their hands, cheered.

"Get comfy, friends," Jürgen said, and then he grabbed his and Nelson's bootleg copy of *Koyaanisqatsi,* which they liked to break out for special hallucinogenic occasions. "I think you're going to enjoy this," he said, sliding it into the DVD player. When the Philip Glass score kicked in, jaws dropped and eyes saucered, and Nelson saw Jürgen grin and give a big thumbs-up.

This was the moment when Lance Riggins and Chelsea Stubbins decided to show up.

It's hard to say if this was the third bad thing or not.

Lance Riggins walked through the apartment door chest out, like he expected a hale and hearty greeting, but his friends were piled like puppies in front of the big screen, their minds being blown by video of an imploding building and the surround sound. One or two of them might have been openly weeping at the beauty of the whole thing, which was the point after all. Chelsea Stubbins edged in behind Lance, peeking around his arm. Nelson saw the golden blond of her hair against her navy-blue parka.

"What's going on here?" Lance said.

Jürgen stepped forward. "They're having a religious experience," he said. "Here, let me take your coats, and help yourselves to the brownies."

Chelsea Stubbins slung her parka over her arm and shook her long hair free and Nelson could see little static lightning bolts arc from strand to strand.

I am tripping balls, he thought. Lance Riggins handed his coat to Jürgen and took a big bite of one of the brownies. "Good stuff."

"Indeed," Jürgen replied. "And for the lady?"

Chelsea Stubbins held up her hand in defense. "I'm not one for sweets," she said.

Nelson's spirit sank to his shoes. He watched Jürgen try again, and receive a second demurral. Nelson couldn't bear it anymore, so he did the final bad thing and went outside to the balcony, the cold air sucking the breath from his lungs to the point they hurt, and then he looked up at the stars.

Whoa, he said to himself. *I am tripping balls.* Vermont had lots and lots of stars, but Utah, somehow, had more. Maybe it was the altitude of Provo or the lack of humidity or the limited light pollution, but from Nelson's balcony, it looked like there were more stars than there was darkness, so the whole firmament was like snow on the television, and that's when Nelson had the visions.

It wasn't clear if the stars were plunging toward him or he was zooming into space, but either way, Nelson was among them. They were impossibly bright, but he, Nelson, could look directly at them. They were impossibly hot, but he, Nelson, could touch them.

Joseph Smith also had visions, which he called revelations because he was founding a religion. While touching the stars, Nelson realized that Joseph Smith might not have been a con man or crazy, but instead might have been tripping balls on some kind of native wacky weed, and this started to change Nelson's perspective on the man, in that Joseph Smith and Nelson had something important in common, namely that they were both capable of traveling in space without a rocket ship. That's got to be an exclusive club.

Nelson waited for his revelation, the message that would catapult him to a raised consciousness and turn him into a leader of men and women across the plains of the country to a promised land where there were so many stars. What a place to guide your people to!

He felt capable of withstanding the skeptics, their slings and arrows —which were literal in the case of Joseph Smith—but would more likely be words in Nelson's. Nelson had withstood these things already, truth be told. Nelson's body swelled with importance as he imagined the multitudes with which he would be filled. Nelson knew Mormons believed that with sufficient devotion and dedication, man could become God, and in that moment, zooming among the stars above, he thought they were probably very wise.

"You're, like, super-high, aren't you?" Chelsea Stubbins said to Nelson.

"I am tripping balls," Nelson replied. He was flat on his back on the concrete slab of the balcony. His eyes were closed, but he sensed a figure looming over him. He knew he was cold, but at the same time couldn't feel it. Maybe he was not flat on his back on a concrete slab but was still floating through space, and Chelsea Stubbins was floating with him. He squeezed his eyes more securely shut in case Chelsea Stubbins speaking to him was a dream.

"It's in the brownies?"

"And the cookies and the Krispies, and everything else," Nelson said.

Nelson heard Chelsea Stubbins put her parka back on before sitting down next to him. The Gore-Tex rubbing was like tires squealing in his ears, and he winced.

"Things feeling a little . . . enhanced?" Chelsea Stubbins asked.

"I am fully alive. I extend to every corner of the universe."

"That sounds like a lot of work."

"I like hearing your voice," Nelson said because it was true. It soothed. "Are you here, or am I there?"

"I'm going to take your hand, OK?" Chelsea Stubbins said.

Nelson nodded, but he was afraid. He didn't think he should be touched under these circumstances, but the warmth of her skin and then her thumb rubbing over the tendons on the back of his hand felt good. He considered opening his eyes, but then reconsidered.

"I'm filled with rage," Nelson said.

"What does that feel like?"

"Bad, mostly. Sometimes good, potentially useful."

"Useful how?"

"Rage has potency, at least that's how it seems."

"You're lucky," Chelsea Stubbins replied. "I got sorrow."

"I don't believe you. You are sunshine."

"It's hard to fathom, I know," Chelsea Stubbins replied. "I didn't believe it myself for a long time." She cupped Nelson's hand in both of hers, applying firm and even pressure. "How's that?" she asked.

It was wonderful. "It's wonderful," Nelson replied. "There are things in this world that are full of wonder, and this is one of them."

Time passed. Maybe eternities, maybe seconds. You can divide every moment into an infinite number of smaller moments, so both those things can be true simultaneously. Nelson concentrated on the one part of his body that felt real, his hand in Chelsea Stubbins's hands. He kept his eyes closed, but he pictured it in his mind perfectly— her blond hair brushing down along the sides of her coat, their breath clouding the air together, their fingers entwined—which felt like the kind of thing only a God could do.

"You seem to know a suspicious amount about drugs," he said.

"Yeah, well . . ."

"Mormons don't take drugs."

"I haven't been Mormon all that long," Chelsea Stubbins replied. "Technically, I'm still a Mormon in training."

Nelson concentrated on keeping his body still even as his heart leapt. Separating Chelsea Stubbins from the Mormonism was going to be cake; the ties binding her to the nonsense were both fresh and weak. "You're going to have to explain," he said.

"We married into it—my mom, I mean. I'm from Jersey originally. I had some issues back there."

"Because of the sorrow," Nelson said.

"That was the start, sure, but then it became its own thing. A greater weight than the sorrow, even."

"I've not experienced that," Nelson said. "I am weightless when I'm like this."

Because in that moment Nelson was so in tune with the world, he could hear Chelsea Stubbins's lips stretch past her teeth as she smiled. "It's different for everybody. You probably have not sucked some guy's dick outside a 7-Eleven for a rock of meth, have you?"

Nelson winced. "I wish you wouldn't talk that way. That was a violence."

"My therapist says it's important to name things as they are, so I try to do that now."

Chelsea Stubbins slid her hands under the sleeve of Nelson's hoodie, rubbing his forearm. "Is that OK?" she asked.

"It's heaven."

"You're coming home."

"I hope not. I like it better here."

"You're a funny kid."

"I'm no kid," Nelson said. "I am a man among men. I have the heart of a stallion and the courage of a lion. I am an unstoppable force combined with an immovable object."

"Then I'm very fortunate to have met you," Chelsea Stubbins said. She removed her hands from under Nelson's hoodie sleeve and moved to straddle him, slowly lowering her entire body on top of Nelson's;

he felt the pressure of her everywhere at once, and he was warm. She turned her head and rested her ear on his chest. Eyes still closed, he breathed deeply and smelled her hair.

"Lilacs," he said. "Just as I figured." Nelson felt her rib cage rise and fall against him. His breath joined hers. "The universe is ordering itself around my thoughts because I am at its center."

"That sounds interesting," Chelsea Stubbins said. "But not necessarily unique."

Nelson wanted to give some thought to this, but not right then.

"Why Lance?" Nelson said. "Surely Lance Riggins does not help with the sorrow. He is no lion. He is a peacock."

Nelson felt her sigh ripple through his body. "No, not really."

"Then why?"

"Sorrow doesn't exist in Lance's world, so I figure maybe it's worth me trying to live there."

"I would use my rage to destroy your sorrow," Nelson said. He was starting to feel the hard concrete of the balcony on his back. "It could not withstand my fury. I would batter it into submission."

"That doesn't sound like a good plan."

"Why not?"

"Don't anger and sadness seem related? Like after you're angry, don't you feel sad?"

Nelson pondered this. He thought about waking up one morning not long before he left home for good, one of the nights he gave as good as he got from his pops. He had a knot above his brow, tender to the touch. He kept kneading it all day, reminding himself it was there. For two days, his father wore a shirt crusted with his own blood thanks to a blow to the nose from Nelson, like some kind of martyr, until Nelson sneaked into the old man's room at night, grabbed it off the floor, and threw it in the laundry.

"It's the smile, isn't it?" Nelson said. "What is up with that? It seems to mean something."

"That's Lance knowing that he belongs to the only true and living church on the face of the whole Earth. He is one of the Chosen, and that joy can barely be contained, and so he smiles," Chelsea said.

"And you believe that?" Nelson felt another sigh, this one longer. It was the sorrow. It waved through him. It felt far more potent than rage.

"I do not, but I would like to, so I'm going to try. They say it comes to you if you let it in."

"Are we breaking up?" Nelson said.

Chelsea laughed into his chest. Is there anything better than a beautiful girl laughing into your chest? Nelson could not think of anything better. "We were never together," she replied.

"Au contraire," Nelson said. He raised his arms, wrapped them fully around Chelsea Stubbins's body and squeezed her to him. "Do you feel how strong I am?"

"I do."

Nelson held Chelsea Stubbins until his arms grew tired, his grip slackened. His whole body was tired. It had been quite a journey.

"I'm leaving soon," Chelsea Stubbins said. "Lance ate a brownie."

"It's not going to work out, you know," Nelson said.

Chelsea Stubbins raised her head from Nelson's chest. He felt her chin press at his sternum and knew that if he opened his eyes, there she'd be, but he did not.

"You're probably right," she said. "I've got my doubts, but it's the plan for now."

"I have nothing," Nelson replied. "I have nothing but a phone that is trying to kill me."

"Life is a disease that only death can cure."

"Who said that?" Nelson asked.

"I'm pretty sure I did."

"You're not the first."

"Nor the last."

"I can make you laugh," Nelson said. "Lance may be filled with joy, but he is without mirth."

This time Chelsea Stubbins nodded into Nelson's chest, her chin digging hard. "He's going to be pissed if he figures out you dosed him."

"I could never be afraid of Lance Riggins."

"I'll tell him it was food poisoning. We had fish tacos before we came."

"What kind of asshole orders fish tacos in Provo, Utah?"

Chelsea Stubbins laughed again.

"You see? See?" Nelson said. He tried to keep the pleading out of his voice. He'd removed that tone a long time ago, when his pops had told him that whiners got no place in the world. "And he has terrible taste in music, I bet."

"Nickelback rules."

Nelson felt some small measure of the rage return. "This is what I'm talking about. It's what's wrong with America."

"Nickelback is Canadian."

"We've infected them too."

"What makes you so sure we're right?" Chelsea Stubbins asked. "Who, exactly, is on top in this world? Where do you see the rage and the sorrow? Doesn't that tell you something?"

"It's just all so ridiculous," Nelson said.

"Isn't it?"

Another of those moments subdivided into smaller and smaller moments passed. Nelson tried to count them.

"I'm getting up," Chelsea Stubbins said. Nelson felt her rise until she was kneeling between his legs. "I think you're OK now," she said "You have Jürgen, and your phone that is trying to kill you. That's something."

Nelson suspected that her kneeling that way in front of him might have been the most beautiful thing he'd ever have a chance to see, but he kept his eyes closed just in case it wasn't, because he couldn't bear to know something like that.

"Will I see you again?" Nelson asked.

"Probably Monday, right? Third shift?"

He nodded at Chelsea Stubbins and raised his hand in farewell, gesturing from the wrist like a king.

Nelson heard the balcony door open; a blast of heated air washed over him. The chant *Ko-Yaa-Nis-Qatsi, Ko-Yaa-Nis-Qatsi* reached out from the living room. Nelson knew on the screen a rocket was exploding, its flaming pieces drifting beautifully to the ground.

My Dog and Me

I've been experiencing dissatisfaction with my dog. As a dog, he's not bad—sleeps at appropriate times, fetches with moderate to high enthusiasm, never messes in the apartment except that one time I temporarily lost track of where we lived and hadn't been home for maybe thirty-six hours. When I walked in and smelled the mess and saw the stain on the carpet, and that one of the couch cushions had been disassembled, he was the one who looked pissed. I couldn't blame him. I'd dropped the ball. That was my bad.

But as a source of artistic inspiration, a muse, if you will, he's substandard. I go to the bookstore a lot, and right near the front, where you can't miss it, there's a whole section of books about dogs. Some of these books are even narrated or apparently written by the dogs themselves. I pretend to be catching up with my tabloids in the magazine aisle while I watch people approach this section with the dog books, and their faces do something really interesting, like their skin is melting off their bones, which sounds gross, but what I mean to say is that they look relaxed, peaceful.

See, if my dog were more inspirational, I wouldn't grab these wrong-sounding metaphors and make people enjoying a private moment of reverie look like ghouls.

In these books the dogs are very busy saving people. Sometimes it's a family, other times a whole town. The titles are all like *[Unusual Dog Name], the Story of a Dog That Saved [Thing That Needed Saving]*. It's a formula, but it must work because just *look* at all these books.

My dog does have a good name for a book title. His name is "Oscar." But *Oscar, the Story of a Dog That Does Just About What You'd Expect a Dog Would Do Most of the Time* doesn't have much of a hook. He does bark whenever he hears the *pchoo-pchoo-pchoo* sound that accompanies someone choosing a Daily Double square. Oscar and I watch *Jeopardy* together every single day, me shouting the answers at the television, him barking at the Daily Double sound. It's something of a highlight for both of us.

The most popular dog-centric books involve this Labrador named Marley who has inspired multiple titles, and even written several on his own for children, all this despite having been dead for quite a few years. Now that's a real trick. Apparently, Marley is famous for teaching a young attractive couple how to love unconditionally so they could be good parents and even better people. In the first Marley book, Marley's owner says, "Marley taught me about living each day with unbridled exuberance and joy, about seizing the moment and following your heart." But I read that book and watched about eighteen minutes of the movie inspired by it, and mostly what I think Marley teaches us is that, as long as you're a dog, you can get away with being a total raging asshole.

You can say a lot of things about my dog, but he's no asshole.

One of the books is about a dog who rescued people from the Twin Towers. Out of patriotic duty I brought that one home, but I don't really want to read it. I have a hunch I'm not alone on that front. My dog never rescued anybody. *Au contraire,* I rescued him, and from his perspective it was a real lottery moment, given the odds, you know, the sheer number of his canine brethren lined up in cages stacked from floor to ceiling at the shelter he called home at the time. I went down a row, peering into each cage at the candidate inside. Some barked viciously, others barked friendlily. Some pressed their noses or paws to the bars. The dark concrete floor had a drain in it, and I knew what that was for. A woman who volunteered at the shelter was following me, offering a kind of color commentary about each of the dogs: "This one likes his belly scratched." "She just loves to cuddle." "He's great with children." I wondered how she knew all this stuff about these dogs. Maybe she took them home for a test drive, like car salesmen will do with the new models so they can speak knowledgeably to customers about handling and acceleration.

I said to her, "Which one goes zero to sixty fastest?"

"We have some greyhounds in the pens outside," she replied, and I realized that once again, I'd made most of the joke in my head. The woman looked like one of those people who used to be really overweight but then got the stomach surgery so they deflate, but what's left is a sort of skin sack that the fatter person used to live in. I admired the sacrifice, the dedication it must have taken to see the process through, but it didn't look good on her.

I figured the woman might be too ugly to love, something I often feared about myself.

A basset hound. That's what she looked like.

Being ugly in the dog world is actually a virtue. The books about the dogs that save things often have pictures of these dogs on the cover and very few are classically handsome. In fact, the odder-looking the dog, the more people it seems to have saved. One of the dog book stars, a pitbull mix, was missing an ear and had a jagged scar circling one eye, like someone had tried to carve the eye out of his head with something simultaneously sharp and dull. This dog had saved himself as well as several others because of his indomitable spirit. Based on his looks, if this dog was a human and an actor, he'd be playing junkies and pederasts exclusively, but at the bookstore I saw one young and pretty girl disengage from the boyfriend whose arm she had been clutching so she could pick up the book and coo at the cover image. *Soooooo cute.*

The barking from all the desperate shelter dogs was like static in my ears and the smell of piss and disinfectant was like static in my nose, and there at the end of the row in a cage at eye height was Oscar. He was sitting upright, mostly alert, looking straight at me. His eyes were and are black, unexpressive, but very, very deep, like two pools of oil. The placard on the cage called him "Fluffy," but I saw through that.

"This one doesn't do much," the woman said.

"I can relate," I said.

She looked at the floor. I figured maybe she could relate too.

"His name is Oscar," I said.

She put some glasses that had been dangling around her neck by a chain up onto her nose and looked at the placard. "Says here that it's Fluffy."

"It's wrong," I said. I pointed at Oscar. "I'll take this one."

"We have several other rooms," she replied. But I couldn't imagine wanting to walk through several other rooms of this.

"He's perfect," I said, but what I probably meant was, *He's good enough.*

I took him home and we began our lives together, and at least until I realized that he's below par as a muse and/or savior, it was pretty good. We had *Jeopardy.* We had walks in the morning and afternoon where people would often look at him and smile and then their eyes would reach up to mine and they'd still be smiling. It was all very *How bad can a guy be with a nice dog like that?*

When I'd weep inexplicably at something showing on the television, he'd leave the room, which I thought I appreciated, as it allowed me a little dignity and privacy, until I realized this behavior was inconsistent with him saving me. I yelled at his retreating back, "You're not doing the job, pal! Not acceptable! You're not showing me anything about how to live life with this walking away business," but nothing stopped the clack of his nails on the wood floor as he retreated to our bedroom.

So· this afternoon, after the walk, and before *Jeopardy,* I decide to read one of the dog books aloud to Oscar, to see if maybe it will provide some inspiration. This one is a real doozy. It's about a man trapped in his house by Hurricane Katrina, and because of swelling in his legs due to the diabetes he can't get out or go for help. For seven days, while he waits for rescue, his two Dobermans scavenge for food and bring it back to the man. It's the perfect kind of book because even in the most desperate parts you sense it's all going to be OK, since no one would publish this book if the man died horribly, maybe even urging the Dobermans to feed on his corpse so they could live.

When Oscar looks like he's about to fall asleep I read louder. When one of the many amazing things happens, I mark my place with a finger and look directly at him and say, "Can you believe this? This is fucking amazing." He seems unimpressed, like he's heard it all before, like in the dog world this story is cliché, mundane.

"Would you rather I read about Marley?" I say.

It's a pretty short book, and reading doesn't take all that long. There's a happy ending, just as I suspected. The man had to have a leg amputated because the dogs couldn't scavenge insulin, but he lived, which is what we're told counts above everything else. He refused to leave the house until the rescuers promised to bring the dogs with. They all live in Alabama now.

After finishing, I look up, and Oscar is indeed sleeping on his side in the daylight slanting through the windows. Almost time for his dinner, then his walk, then *Jeopardy*, then more television, then bed.

"It's about the loyalty, pal," I say. "Man's best friend." Still on his side, Oscar stretches and grunts and blows air out of his cheeks, which is one of the more endearing things he does. He rolls from his side to his belly and rises to his haunches like a yogi.

"Would you do for me what those dogs did for that man?" I say. "Would you save me like I saved you?" He stands and yawns and shakes the sleep out of his head, his ears thwapping.

Oscar has also noticed that it is near dusk. He walks into the kitchen area and sits next to the cabinet where we keep the food. He does this sometimes.

Who am I kidding? He does this every day.

"Have I ever forgotten?" I say. He looks back at me with those bottomless eyes.

"Except the one time, I mean, which I've apologized for." He lies down in front of the cabinet, chin on his paws. I see myself on the couch reflected distantly in his eyes.

"What are you teaching me about life and living?" I say. "Tell me." His tail swishes the air behind him, stirring some dust motes. When he's really excited, his tail takes the shape of a comma arcing over his back. My dog doesn't speak, or write, or even inspire books, but in this moment I think I get the message.

This is next, he is saying. *Life is about whatever you do next.*

Return-to-Sensibility Problems after Penetrating Captive Bolt Stunning of Cattle in Commercial Beef Slaughter Plant #5867: Confidential Report

Purpose

To evaluate the efficacy of penetrating captive bolt stunning of cattle in Commercial Beef Slaughter Plant #5867 and identify potential causes of a return to sensibility among stunned cattle.

Purpose behind the Purpose

Stifling the complaints. In the opinion of this researcher, the combination of on-site protests; undercover, illegally obtained video aired on one of the TV newsmagazines with a title dealing with either time or vision (this researcher forgets which); a rising sense of public outrage; and, most important, lawsuits, results in the drawer of the short straw (that being this researcher) trading his oxfords for work boots, his pleated wool trousers for rubber coveralls, and spending sixteen consecutive days on the slaughter floor at plant #5867.

Procedure

184 hours of stunning over 16 operating days were observed at an average line speed of 129 cattle/hr. Cattle were evaluated for signs of returning to sensibility on the bleed rail.

Why You've Got to Hang Them on the Bleed Rail Prior to Evaluation of Proper Stunning

1. Because if they aren't stunned, they are more than willing to drive a stone-hard hoof through your skull.

2. Helps avoid misinterpretation of spasms that occur during ejection from the conveyor restrainer system and of tonic spasms, commonly seen a few seconds after stunning.

Procedure cont.

Previous research suggests that the corneal reflex becomes absent in conjunction with electroencephalographic patterns that indicate the animal is insensible. Cattle no longer have corneal reflexes when all of the following four criteria are fulfilled.

1. No spontaneous blinking

2. No vocalization
   a. Mooing
   b. Bellowing
   c. Or any other sound

3. Eyes have a wide, blank stare; the eyeballs must not be rotated; and nystagmus must be absent.

4. No righting reflex when the animal is hung on the bleed rail. Animal must:

a. Have straight back
b. Neck and head will be limp and flaccid
c. Momentary flopping of a limp, loose head should not mistaken for a righting reflex, and kicking and limb movement must be ignored.

How You Come to Ignore Kicking and Limb Movement of a Cow or Bull Recently Stunned and Hung on a Bleed Rail

If you see anything enough times over and over and over, that anything, no matter what it is, becomes entirely unexceptional. Plus, sometimes they just twitch for awhile.

Procedure cont.

In addition to the previous four criteria, if the tongue is fully extended, limp, and flaccid, the animal can be considered properly stunned and insensible, as in the author's experience, an animal with a fully extended, limp, and flaccid tongue will never ever never have spontaneous blinking.

A completely relaxed jaw is also a good indicator of profound brain dysfunction.

A Note on the Smell inside Commercial Beef Slaughtering Plant #5867

Thick. Tactile almost, like you could reach out and hold it in your fist. Like it surrounds you. In this researcher's experience, an adjective such as "chewy" would not be entirely out of the question. The dominant scent is fresh cow insides, which this researcher suggests smell exactly as you think they would.

Procedure cont.

However, a stiff curled tongue is a sign of possible return to sensibility.

On the other hand, the tongue will not always slip out of the jaw, even in properly stunned cattle.

Thus, if the tongue is fully extended, limp, and flaccid, one can conclude that the animal is insensible, but the *absence* of a fully extended, limp, and flaccid tongue *should not* be used as an indicator of return to sensibility.

I'm not sure what that means either.

A Note on Where the Wife of This Researcher Believes His "Fieldwork" Boots Should Be Kept during His Project at Commercial Beef Slaughter Plant #5867

Outside. Far away from the house, inside a plastic bag, buried in a hole. A ditch, inside a plastic bag, buried in a ditch outside, far, far away from the house. Far, far away from the house, inside a plastic bag, buried in a ditch lined with vulcanized sheeting and sprinkled with lime, outside.

False Signs of a Return to Sensibility

The tail may move, or raise, or twitch, even when animals are insensible. When the animal is hung on the bleed rail, the tail gradually becomes limp and lies down flat against the rump.

Occasionally, insensible cattle with the limp head, blank stare, and extended, limp, and flaccid tongue will withdraw the forelimb if a person grabs it; therefore a reflex reaction to a tactile stimulus of a limb is not considered a sign of sensibility.

What "Stunned" Means in the Context of This Report

Dead. Brain-dead. Absence of neurological functioning.

The Best Word to Describe What It's Like When You Grab the Forelimb of a Seemingly Stunned Cattle Hanging from a Bleed Rail and It Pulls Away

Spooky.

The Company's Official Policy on Hanging a Fully Sensible, Unstunned Animal on the Bleed Rail

We have zero tolerance for the inhumane treatment of animals used in our products. We pledge to you, the consumer, that all animals are fed, housed, and slaughtered according to the most stringent of USDA guidelines as outlined in the Humane Slaughter Act of 2001.

Procedure cont.

If a problem with return to sensibility was observed, additional data were collected, as time permitted, to identify the cause. Alternatively, follow-up interviews with staff were conducted to identify the cause of the return-to-sensibility problem.

A Note on the Dreams of the Researcher Investigating the Return-to-Sensibility Problems after Penetrating Captive Bolt Stunning of Cattle in Commercial Beef Slaughter Plant #5867

Night-long, slow-motion scenes of traumas the researcher is sure never happened to him in his waking life. In one, the researcher is a boy, and he hugs an iron bedpost, legs and arms wrapped around it seemingly multiple times, like his arms are spaghetti tensileness, and he looks over his shoulder at a man who resembles his father, but is larger through the chest, advancing toward him with a belt looped once, forming a strop that the man knocks against his palm.

Word Carved into the Paint of the Researcher's Chrysler Conquest, Presumably by One of the Protestors

Beast!

Results

In all, 23,736 cows and bulls were observed, and 284 (1.2%) had signs of returning to sensibility after hanging on the bleed rail. Cattle that were *obviously* not insensible after a single shot and were restunned prior to hoisting were not tabulated as they are outside the immediate scope of this research, but this researcher estimates their number to be in excess of 1,000, of which a small percentage required more than a second stunning.

Processing Steps Following the Bleed Rail Hanging

Bleeding, leg removal, skinning, scalding, head removal, and chemical dehairing, among others.

Results cont.

The most common indicator of animals returning to sensibility after hanging on the bleed rail consisted of movement of the tongue out and then back in and twitching of the nose. In a single case (#4557), tongue movement, puffing of the cheeks, vocalization (mooing, bellowing, low moaning, and squeals), limb movement (thrashing, really), and twitching of the nose were all present even after multiple (9) restunning attempts.

Partial Transcript of Conversation between This Researcher and One of the Female Protestors Held through a Closed Car Window as This Researcher Waited for the Security Gate to Open

PROTESTOR: I see you! You're being judged! I am judging you!

RESEARCHER: Please, I'm just trying to . . . can you move back?

PROTESTOR: How many today? How many dead today? How many killed?

RESEARCHER: Please, I just want to get through.

PROTESTOR: I know your name. I know where you live. You have children!

RESEARCHER: Is that a threat?

PROTESTOR: It is what it is.

Results cont.

The leading indicator of a potential return-to-sensibility problem was "soft-sounding" shots, which may be an indicator of an underpowered stunner. Further investigation revealed that cartridges for the stunner were stored in a damp supply room near the slaughter floor, thus causing a certain percentage of shots that fall below the effective bolt speed of 65m/s.

Percentage of Surfaces inside Commercial Beef Slaughter Plant #5867 That Could Be Characterized as "Damp"

100.

Results cont.

Other prevalent causes for the failure to render animals insensible with a single stunner shot included: bent firing pins, stunner damage (case #4557), improper stunner maintenance, dirty stunner trigger, and inexperienced operation (case #4557).

A Question Concerning His Project at Commercial Beef Slaughter Plant #5867 Asked by His Daughter That This Researcher Was Unable to Answer

Do cows have names that they call each other in cow language?

Impressions of the Overall Hygiene/Grooming Practices of the Most "Aggressive" (Female) Protestor

Braless for sure. Each morning as she rushed the car, waving her sign and yelling, her breasts banged into each other beneath her loose peasant blouse. Once, as she pounded a fist on the hood of this researcher's car, this researcher caught a glimpse of a thick thatch of hair at her pit. She was plain and beautiful. Pure. Her scent is unknown. The plant really obliterated everything around. Has the researcher spoken of that already?

What the Nose Movements of This Researcher's Wife Would Say When This Researcher Returns Home from the Plant If Those Nose Movements Were Translated into Verbal Communication

That's strange. What is that? Do you smell something? Yes? Is that a good smell or a horrible smell? Horrible, definitely horrible. Is that really coming from my husband? It is!

Results cont.

Further investigation suggested that the stunner was probably damaged when the cocking mechanism struck the side of the stunning box, as can happen when the rod sticks in the animal's head and the stunner is jerked out of the operator's hand. Careful maintenance of the rubber bumpers that retract the rod can help prevent the rod from sticking in the head.

Abnormal, overly thick skulls can also be blamed for return-to-sensibility problems in a small handful of cases, most notably case #4557.

One of the Things That the Researcher No Longer Takes Pleasure in Following His Experiences at Commercial Beef Slaughter Plant #5867

You were thinking meat, but no, believe it or not, it's television. Like a lot of Americans, this researcher used to find television soothing, particularly at the end of the day, once the kids were down and it was just the researcher and his wife on the couch, watching some show where nothing important would happen, but it was a real pleasure to watch those unimportant things happening. Lately, these people on the screen make him angry and he fidgets and makes sighing noises that annoy his wife.

Interview Summary of Roy L. Clampsin, Line Foreman

Mr. Clampsin recently began his twenty-third year at Plant #5867, and has spent the past seven years as foreman of the stunning/bleeding operation. Mr. Clampsin believes that in his time at Plant #5867 he has "seen it all" and that this researcher was about the "millionth" of "his kind" to "come sniffing around."

When questioned about the possibility of storing the replacement stunner cartridges in the relatively dry front office, Mr. Clampsin asked the researcher if he was a "company man" or a "narc." When informed that this researcher is employed by the company, Mr. Clampsin responded that no one he was acquainted with was going to "traipse over to the next county past hell and gone and take a hit on the production quota just so every last one of next week's hamburgers has its brains scrambled right."

A Word This Researcher Has Been Thinking About a Lot Lately

Cleave. Once the cattle are stunned and hung on the bleed rail they are cleaved apart, by hand, because there is no machine that can do it with the speed and precision necessary, given the inherent variation among cattle. Robots can build cars, but they can't render meat. The thing about cleave, though, is that the word means two opposite things at once. It means to split apart, but also it means "to cling to." How can two things be the same thing, but also their opposites?

Apparent Sharpness of the Knife Used by Roy Clampsin to Remedy Case #4557 of Improper Stunning Prior to Hanging on the Bleed Rail

You just wouldn't believe.

Where Foreman Clampsin Acquired the Nonstandard, Policy-Violating Knife Used to Remedy Case #4557 of Improper Stunning Prior to Hanging on the Bleed Rail

"Nam."

What "Stunned" Meant in a Different Context at One Time

A time, before this researcher was married, when he and his future wife lived in the apartment without much furniture, the one with the large, southeast-facing sliding glass doors that allowed the sun to flood inside and warm the worn wood floors so in the mornings she would stand barefoot, looking out, sipping a cup of tea, and this researcher was behind her looking at her body bared through her nightclothes by the sun and he held his breath so it would not catch in his throat and make a noise that would disturb the picture in front of him.

Partial Interview Transcript of Terry Lobegel, Stunner Operator during Case #4557

Q: How long had you been operating the stunner, and where had you worked previously within the plant?

A: I spent most of the time at the sluicer end, and that is a place you do not want to spend much time. It takes one of two things to get to the stunner floor: seniority, or a union leadership position, of which I had neither. Fortunately, there is a third way, and that way is having dirty pictures of the plant manager having sex with a woman who is not his wife which I had several copies of, as well as the negatives. I also have a computer, scanner, and the plant manager's e-mail address. My wife knows how to work all that stuff. You do the math.

Q: In your own words, please recount the incident involving Case #4557.

A: Here's the deal. Running the stunner wasn't as straightforward as raking entrails down the sluicer bins, but it seemed simple enough: cow comes in, head gets clamped, aim the bolt, and fire away. Simple as pie, seemingly. Turns out it's more art than science.

Q: Can you amplify what you mean by "more art than science?"

A: Amplify? Say it louder? Is the tape not working? Check! Check! One two! How's that?

Q: (Unintelligible)

A: Anyway, these cows are like snowflakes. Looking at a whole field of them you'd be hard-pressed to notice any individual number, but it turns out that no two are quite exactly alike, so while the diagrams on where to aim the stunner and the training video and the guidelines on how much pressure to apply are all well and good, it isn't that simple. Every one has a soft spot, and a millimeter can really make a difference, and the experienced guys just know how to do it. Clampsin warned me it wasn't as easy as it looked, but

I was desperate to get out of that sluicer. Sluicer ain't fit for your worst enemy. My mama always said I'm my own worst enemy, though, so maybe me being back there makes a lot of sense.

Conversation between Researcher and His Wife in Bed the Night after the Incident Involving Case #4557

WIFE: Are you cold?

RESEARCHER: No.

WIFE: Why are you shaking?

RESEARCHER: (No response)

WIFE: Are you OK?

RESEARCHER: (No response)

WIFE: Are you crying?

Why the Blood Can Arc So High and Far Following the Knife's Slash (Partial Transcript of Foreman Roy Clampsin Interview, unedited)

Come here, let me show you something. I said, come here! If you're going to get sick, just get sick; it'll all wash down into the same place. Happens all the time. Bend over. Hold your knees, breathe deep. That's it. Now, come here. Look at that. Big as a basketball, practically. That's that big bastard's heart. And the blood. The blood was coming out of a high-pressure artery, and when you think about it, he'd just survived a murder attempt, so you can bet that that fucker was pumping big-time. You ever been to the drag races and seen an oil line blow when one of them dragsters is coming off the line? It's kind of like that. Shit's amazing, isn't it? Could you imagine such a thing?

Legible Portion of Note Left beneath Researcher's Windshield Wiper, Presumably by Female Protestor a Couple Days after Confronting the Researcher on His Way inside the Plant

. . . about the kids is because I wanted you to think about the world we're going to leave behind, not because I'd do anything to hurt anyone. I do this because I don't want anyone getting hurt. You think I look like a fool, but whose [*sic*] the foolish one?

Interview Summary of Foreman Roy Clampsin cont.

In my experience, people like to kick up a lot of fuss, and the ones who kick up the most fuss, in general, don't know shit about shit. That whole fucking war they sent me to was fuss after fuss, and not a goddamned soul knew fuck-all about it, but everyone had an opinion anyway, and for the most part, same is true here. People just do not want to know about this shit, perfect case in point being you. You wouldn't be here if those hippies hadn't gotten their hemp undies in a bunch, that look on your face makes that plain as day. Not that I blame anyone. Apparently, people more important than me have declared that this is "necessary," so here I am, which is kind of the story of my life.

My daddy always said that "Choices have consequences and bad choices have bad consequences." First time he said it was after I spent my Christmas money on some plastic piece-of-shit toy that Daddy had warned me would fall apart before I got home and did indeed break when I dropped it on the ground exiting the car. The last time was after I'd wrapped my car around an oak, which I'd done because I'd lost the girl I loved and drank too much over the sorrow, and that's what got me kicked out of college once and for all, which is how the army got their hands on me. When I left for basic, I said good-bye to Daddy, who was sitting at the kitchen table reading the paper, and he said, without looking up, "It's been nice knowing you," which I choose to think meant he was worried about what was going to happen to me over there, rather than something else.

So what I'm saying is that I've learned how to live with the consequences of my choices, but what *this* place is about is the consequences of other people's choices, which is the messed-up part. Those hippies are a pain in the ass and I don't like having to wash off the cow shit they throw at my car every morning, and I'm not trying to argue that there's an equivalence between what went on during that war, or any other war and what's going on here, but you've got to admit, they have a point.

Discussion

After firsthand observation of 16 operating days it has been determined that Plant #5867 operates within acceptable tolerances and practices for the safe and humane processing of commercial beef cattle.

The Five Nicest Things the Researcher's Wife Ever Said to Him in Chronological, Rather Than Rank, Order

Ewww, I never slept with Barry!
I love you too.
I do.
I think your shirt's on backwards.
You don't have to go back if you don't want to. We'll be fine.

Discussion cont.

This is not to say that practices and procedures could not be improved, because the ways (if not the means) Plant #5867 could be improved are almost too numerous to list, and yet this researcher finds himself at a loss as to where to begin. This researcher's experiences at Commercial

Beef Slaughter Plant #5867 have reinforced the notion that when it comes to judging things, it's the standard by which we're judging that matters most. This researcher has been to his share of grade school music recitals, and no one would mistake what goes on there for true artistry, and yet the "music" can and does bring the audience to tears. We call the gap between perfection and acceptability the "tolerance." That's another interesting word, isn't it? How tolerant are we, really? Are we tolerant of the right things?

Last Words from the Female Protestor to this Researcher Following His Final Day of On-Site Investigation at Commercial Beef Slaughter Plant #5867

"Take care."

Discussion (cont.)

The thing is, if we're going to do this, there's only so much you can do. What I'm saying is that it is what it is.

Conclusions and Clinical Relevance

Care should be taken to ensure proper stunner maintenance. Stunners should be used correctly, particularly when stunning cows and bulls with heavy skulls.

Monkey and Man

So I was sitting on the couch, scratching behind the dog's second-favorite ear and humming a song of woe over Constance leaving us, when the doorbell rang. Through the cracked door I saw a vaguely familiar monkey dressed in tuxedo shirt, bow tie, and cummerbund, but no pants. He clutched a circular hatbox.

"Sorry, no monkeys needed here," I said.

But the monkey jammed the hatbox in the closing door, and a hairy paw extended through the opening. The paw held a convincing replica of my wallet, so convincing that it and my wallet appeared to be one and the same.

He said, "You need this; we're going for a ride. Giuseppe is dead."

Giuseppe, the organ-grinder, dead, and this, his monkey.

He stepped inside, opened the hatbox, and changed into an outfit of cutoff shorts held up by rainbow suspenders before folding the tuxedo top neatly back into the box. His chest was sunken and only spotted with fur. He was an old monkey.

"Where did you get this?" I said, searching through the wallet, cataloguing the contents. The dog circled, showed just a hint of teeth.

The monkey sighed. "Have you noticed that when you're arguing with your now ex-girlfriend, you are often distracted by the hot flush of her cheeks? Of course I know you are, because you never felt the light touch of my deft monkey paw."

"All the money is gone." It was.

"I hardly think that seven dollars is something to quibble over when one has been reunited with his wallet." He snapped the hatbox's latch closed and flipped on the television. Over the news anchor's shoulder was a file picture of Giuseppe in his fez and fringed jacket, squeezing his accordion. In the picture, the monkey perched on his shoulder, grinning and clapping.

The monkey looked at the TV. "Did you know," he said, "that when an animal shows its teeth, that's a sign of aggression? For some reason you people take it as smiling."

The dog worked into a growl. The monkey shushed him, flashing the back of his paw. He removed a small steno-style notebook and pencil from the hatbox, licked the pencil tip, and jotted a few things down. As the news bulletin ended, the monkey underlined the last bit of his entry and snapped the notebook shut before turning to face me.

"I want to prepare you for a couple of things," he said, a replica of concern crossing his simian face. "Thing the first is that it's possible, nay, probable, check that, definite, that Constance has already moved on from the relationship."

"And the second?"

"The second is that you may be a suspect in Giuseppe's death, given that your thumbprint is on his throat and he did indeed die of strangulation."

I started to speak, but the monkey placed his long, bony finger across my lips.

"She is a beauty, for sure, but she is not right for you." He took his finger from my lips and poked the roll of flab at my waist. "Look at this," he said. "Should she be subjected to that? And this," he said, turning me to face the hall mirror. "Seriously, it's important that you stick to your own kind, your own level."

"I didn't kill Giuseppe," I said.

"That's good," he said. "Go with that. Very convincing. Now, let's go clear your name."

"Why do you care?"

"I am but a simple monkey who exists to serve my humankind brethren as I have done for all my days, but also, from your wallet,

I noticed that you are a midlevel supervisor at a shipping company, which will come in handy when it's time for you to express your gratitude for not going to jail for the rest of your life. Now, let's get going, because any second the cops are going to show up and ask questions you can't answer, which is going to make you look really suspicious, and if you're locked up, you're never going to be able to prove yourself innocent."

"But I *am* innocent," I told the monkey.

"Don't overdo it," the monkey said. "It'll get stale." The monkey hitched his thumbs under his rainbow suspenders and hoisted his cutoffs above his jutting hip bones. "And leave the creature here," he said, pointing at the dog. "I don't know how you can stand the smell."

As I pulled my coat off the rack, the monkey clambered up my leg to the top of the stand and grabbed a baseball hat that he jammed onto my head and low over my eyes. "We don't need anyone recognizing you," he said.

I opened the door and the monkey craned his head through the opening for a couple seconds. "Follow," he said.

And I did. What can I say? He was a very persuasive monkey.

In the car, driving the tollway, I scanned for police heading the other way. The monkey sat boosted on the hatbox and fingered the cheap plastic beads dangling from the review, baubles showered on Constance for flashing her breasts at a street fair.

"These are nice," the monkey said before letting go the beads and placing his paw on my leg.

I never particularly liked displaying them there, given how they were procured, but Constance insisted, saying I shouldn't be jealous since I was the only one who got to do more than just look.

Or not, if this monkey was right.

As we approached the tollbooth, I fished in the ashtray for the appropriate change, but the monkey grabbed my hand, then stood briefly and from the hatbox pulled a metal slug with a string tied through the hole. I rolled down the window, the monkey fired the slug into the basket, waited momentarily, then yo-yoed the slug back into his paw.

The light flashed green, the toll gate rose, and the monkey gave me a look that said, "What are you waiting for?"

We pulled slowly through. I looked around, but nobody said a word. We accelerated back to speed.

This monkey was creeping me out. He was obviously some kind of con monkey, but on the other hand, he'd been right about more than a couple of things. I'd never been entirely sure that Constance felt about me the way I felt about her, which was a kind of soul ache, a desperate helplessness every time I thought about her. When I would mention things like cohabitation, even marriage, she would laugh, not a mean laugh, necessarily, but her teeth would flash and there would be something in her eyes asking if I was kidding, implying that I was only temporary, that an attempt to move closer would push her further away like two magnets turned to the same poles.

I had a test of my love for Constance. When she was not there, I would sit on my couch and turn on the cable news and wait for the first report of a tragedy (it usually didn't take long), a plane crash in Phuket, an overturned trawler in the Bering Sea, brushfires, E. coli, West Nile, car bomb, falling into the polar bear enclosure at the zoo, what have you, and I would imagine it was Constance on that plane or ship, or hospital bed, or hanging from a polar bear's jaws being dragged, unconscious and limp, into its den, and as I imagined this, her face pained and confused, her body battered, I would search my feelings and feel only devastation. I would literally wish to trade places with her, at the bottom of icy ocean, or in a million bloody pieces spread across a road, or again, what have you, and in those moments I knew for sure that what I felt for Constance had to be love.

Once, after we had made love, I had turned to Constance and stroked her sweat-matted hair out of her eyes and asked what she would do if I died and she said, "I'm sleepy."

* * *

"You know, of course," the monkey said, "that you and I share 98 percent of our genetic material."

"I guess so."

"Ninety-eight percent!" he practically shouted. "That precious dog of yours, 60, 65 percent tops, yet he is treated like royalty. You and me, we're almost the same, virtually identical, and look what you do to us? You keep us in cages. You rub cosmetics on our skin to see if we break out in welts. You inject us with medicines to see if our hearts explode or our kidneys shrivel or our stomachs ulcer. You enclose us in plexiglas and give us ropes to swing on and a deflated soccer ball to kick around and you watch and point and giggle as we make sweet monkey love to each other, and yet you wonder why we fling our poop back at you and screech and beat our chests. You strap tiny cymbals on our paws and demand that we clap along with your stupid three songs, all of which are in goddamn waltz time and for that we are fed cat food and sleep in a drawer. Can you imagine the rage? Can you?"

I could see that the organ-grinder's monkey was not observing safety protocol and wearing his seatbelt. He was standing excitedly on the hatbox and banging his little fist against the dash to punctuate his words. I eased my foot deeper into the gas pedal and pictured throwing on the brake and watching his body launch through my windshield, a monkey missile that I might or might not drive over as I passed.

"Don't do it," the monkey said.

"What?"

"What you're thinking; don't do it."

"I'm not thinking anything."

The monkey idly scratched his wrinkled ballsack through the leg of his cutoff shorts. He looked at me intently, batting his long monkey lashes. "Don't fucking do it," he said. "Don't even think it. You *need* me."

He sat back down on the hatbox and for a while we were both silent, until he raised his arm and pointed.

"Look, up there, in the distance," the monkey said. "Look at how narrow the road is, like a sliver could not slide through, yet, as I approach, it widens, opening itself to me."

The monkey gripped my hand as we walked toward our historic downtown. "Look both ways," he said as we crossed the street. Ours is a good downtown, clean, gentrified but still charming, cobblestone streets and gas lighting mixed with shiny boutiques and restaurants with white tablecloths. Our steel drummers and Pan flautists and organ grinders are licensed and bonded, and apparent stranglings are not even a semi-regular occurrence. As we neared the center square I could see orange cones with yellow tape stretched between them cordoning off the area where Giuseppe was found, his usual spot. A group of people knotted at the scene, sharing shrugs. I started to walk toward them, but the monkey tugged me away.

"You don't want to return to the scene of the crime," he said. "Very suspicious."

"But I wasn't there to begin with."

"Once again, I remind you of the thumbprint, not to mention the slip of paper in his back pocket with your address and phone number on it. Clearly you two had a connection. Now you need some money. Thank God you got your wallet back."

The monkey tugged me over to a street ATM and gestured toward the screen. The machine sucked my card inside, and I blocked the monkey from the keyboard as I punched in my code, but as I glanced over my shoulder I saw that he wasn't even looking at me and instead scanned the street, lightly hopping from one foot to the other.

"Hey," the monkey said as I slipped the money into my wallet and reclaimed my card. "I bet I can tell you where you got your shoes at."

I looked down at my shoes, nondescript brown loafers, bought at Constance's insistence that I, for once, spend more than thirty dollars on shoes. I remembered the day, her squeezing my arm in encouragement as I flipped my credit card across the counter. They were great shoes, comfortable. Durable. Swedish. Available just about anywhere.

I'm not stupid. I was suspicious. "How could you possibly know where I got my shoes?"

"I just do."

"I don't believe you."

"Do you not believe me two hundred bucks' worth?"

I was already out seven bucks and a potential murder rap to this monkey. I was Constanceless. What else was there to lose, other than a couple hundred bucks? "You're on," I said.

"You got them on your feet," he said.

"What?"

"Your feet—you got them on your feet."

"I don't get it," I said.

The monkey cupped his elbow in one hand and used the other to massage his temple. "I said, 'I bet I can tell you where you got your shoes at,' and you said, 'You're on,' for two hundred bucks, no less, and I said, 'You got them on your feet,' which is 100 percent true, which means you owe me the double c-note."

I'd had just about enough of this monkey. "That's stupid, and I'm not paying."

"Too late," the monkey said, snapping his fingers and flashing a roll of twenties. I pulled out my wallet and looked inside. All the money I'd withdrawn from the ATM was gone. "That was three hundred."

"Interest," the monkey said, grabbing my arm and once again tugging me down the street toward wherever we were going next.

"Now," he said, speaking as we walked, or rather I walked and he waddled along next to me, bowlegged, shambling. "This next part is going to be hard for you, but it's a sort of bad news, good news thing and I've really already told you the bad news."

"Which part was that?"

"The part that Constance is not right for you and that she's already moved on to someone else. That's true, and you're about to be confronted with incontrovertible evidence of it, which will likely be painful because you humans are irrational creatures who hold onto beliefs despite all signs to the contrary. The irrational belief in this instance being that Constance might have ever loved you, just in case I'm not being clear."

I was getting pretty fucking tired of this monkey. This was a seriously annoying monkey. I understood that pound for pound, monkeys are many times stronger than human beings, but as he shuffled beside me, in my hand, he felt weightless, like with a single movement I could spin like a discus thrower and hurl him far, far away. "What's the good news?" I said.

"The good news is that you are about to be a witness to her own heartbreak as she is about to be rejected by the one she chose over you."

"How do you know this?"

"I know it because I know it, and I know this also: that when you see Constance having her heart broken you will know yourself whether or not you *really* did love her."

"What do you mean?"

"You'll see," he said, letting go of my hand and pointing at a restaurant window across the street. Constance was there visible through the window, sitting alone at a table for two like she was on display. She wore the blue dress. A single candle enclosed in glass flickered from the middle of the table. There was a bottle of wine with two glasses, one empty, hers half-full. My heart leapt into my throat and merged with the rising bile. This felt like love to me. Was this what the monkey was talking about?

The monkey skittered toward the restaurant door. Constance peered out the window and looked right at me and smiled. She raised her hand and waved her fingers, but I could see her eyes were tracking something other than me.

As the monkey approached the door, the hostess swung it open and the monkey skipped through, disappearing briefly before clambering up onto the chair across from Constance and then all the way to the tabletop. Constance offered her cheek, and the monkey pecked at her with his lips. A waiter appeared and poured wine into the empty glass. The monkey gripped it in both hands and took an overlong swallow. Constance beamed at him. I'd never seen her look so beautiful.

The monkey squatted, perched on his edge of the table, and did almost all the talking, whatever he was saying briefly punctuated by single words from Constance. Even from a distance I could see her grow flushed and agitated, her bottom lifting off the chair as she stood to protest the monkey's message. The news was clearly not good, and she wasn't having it. I'd never seen her so worked up, but after a few final words from the monkey she slumped backwards, grabbing the wineglass and draining the last of it before reaching for the bottle and refilling her glass to the top. The monkey moved to her side of the table and touched his hand briefly to her cheek, wiping away what I imagined was a tear. He flipped a trio of twenties onto the table before hopping back down, and out the restaurant door, re-crossing the street toward me. Constance stood and pressed her face and hands to the window, watching the monkey retreat. She pounded against the glass and shouted, "Come back! Wait! Come back!" until a waiter pulled her away. The monkey never turned around, even when he arrived at my side. My fists clenched and pulsed.

"I ought to kill you," I said.

"Why?"

Why, indeed? Why for the second time in a few hours was I thinking about how I might kill this monkey, how I could quite possibly grab one arm and one leg and pull as hard as I could, rending him into pieces? "You took her from me."

"Is that really why?"

"Yes."

The monkey sighed and shook his head sadly. "Then you never loved her either, my friend. That's not love; that's possession. If you loved her, you would want to kill me because I've just broken her heart and you would not be able to bear that." The monkey jerked his thumb over his shoulder at Constance, who had broken away and angrily waved the near-empty bottle of wine at the waitstaff that now surrounded her table. Sirens began softly calling in the distance. The monkey's ears pricked.

"Time to go," he said.

We drove toward the shipping-terminal offices, but the monkey couldn't manage to be quiet. "About that DNA business," he said, "they always talk about the monkeys' share of human DNA, like you all are the ideal and we are the simulacrum. But why can't it be the other way around? Why can't it be that humans have 98 percent of monkeys' DNA?"

"Maybe because monkeys didn't discover DNA," I replied. I was still pissed at this monkey, maybe even more pissed than before, since I was starting to feel like he might've been right about me and Constance. I drove fast, recklessly, steering toward potholes, feeling the tires spin in the air as we'd launch over the bumps. The monkey took no notice. I considered turning off the headlights to see what that might be like, if a surprise telephone pole might crop up in front of the car's grille.

"Seriously," he said, "think about it. You have something we don't, the whole opposable thumb thing, but in return we have things you don't, our own 2 percent."

"I suppose that's true."

"Of course it's true."

"OK."

"And I'm pretty sure I know what it is."

"What?"

"What we have that you don't."

"What's that?"

The monkey stared out the window. I could see his reflection in the glass, his eyes flicking across the rows of trees that lined the road. "You're not going to believe me."

"No," I said, "probably not."

"I deserved that," he said. "You're mad, and I don't blame you. I don't expect you to ever forgive me, but I think someday you'll realize that this is all for the best."

"Hmph."

"You know," he said, still gazing out the window, "I've never climbed anything higher than a coat stand. I've never caught or picked my own food. I'm not even sure what I'm supposed to eat." His voice trailed off, and I thought maybe he was going to shut up for the rest of the ride to the depot, but then he cleared his throat with a loud hack and started in again.

"I'm a wild animal who's barely been outside! First the lab, then Giuseppe . . . but here's the thing. I *do* know what it's like to climb hand over foot, sixty feet up into the canopy, and make the blind leap from one tree or branch or vine to another, just knowing without *really* knowing that something is going to be there to grab on to. I can *feel* it in every part of me. If you gave me a tree and some vines I could do it, *just like that.*" The monkey tapped his knuckles against the glass to emphasize the last three words. "Though I never met her, I know my grandmother's smell and her mother's smell, and so on and so on, back and back. I've never done it, but I'm certain I could comb the mites out of another monkey's fur with my fingers. I'm pretty sure that there's someplace where the night sky is so clear that when you look up there's so many stars that it looks cloudy. I think that after a rain you can suck the water from the grass, and you've never tasted anything so pure."

Even in the car window's reflection I could see the tears running down his cheeks.

"There's a lot of time to think when you're chained to an organ grinder with nothing to do but clap your tiny cymbals together and steal the occasional passerby's wallet, and what I've come to realize is that within me I carry everything of my ancestors, that I can feel every last bit of them, that I am the sum total of each and every one of them, all the way back to whenever it was that we were all together—your kind and my kind—and some of us thought it would be a good idea to stand upright and leave our genitals open to attack. Anyway, I think that's what's different between your kind and mine."

The monkey snuffled and rubbed his arm across his nose.

"What is it that you want?" I said.

"I want to go home, but I don't know where that is. Do you know where that is?"

"I don't know," I said. "Africa?"

The monkey mouthed the word, *Africa*, as though he were tasting it. "I don't think *we* call it that, but it sounds right. Send me to Africa."

We used the last of the money I'd taken from the ATM to buy provisions out of the depot vending machine. I wrote FRAGILE, THIS SIDE UP on each side of the shipping container and punched air holes in the sides. I placed the sodas, candy, chips, and boxed sandwiches inside. "That should be plenty," I said. The monkey set the hatbox on the floor and stepped out of the cutoffs and rainbow suspenders. Carefully he folded the clothes and put them back inside the hatbox before handing it to me.

"Won't you get cold?" I said.

"I think," he said, "when it gets cold we huddle together for warmth. I'm looking forward to that." The monkey extended his paw to me, and I shook it before he climbed inside the container, his head just barely poking out of the top.

"Wait," I said. "What about Giuseppe?"

The monkey reached out and tapped a bony finger on the hatbox. "Just give the cops this. It spells out everything. The toxicology and my confession will tell the tale. Farewell, friend." The monkey squatted in the container and I sealed the top with tape. As I left the depot, I could hear the crinkle of a candy bar being unwrapped, followed by some noisy chewing. "Farewell, monkey," I said, snapping off the lights.

At home, despite it being pretty late, the dog was waiting at the door for me with his ball. Across the street from our apartment is a ball field that is lighted at night for the neighborhood kids to use. Three or four of them sprinted around the bases, taking turns sliding into home, seeing who could kick up the biggest cloud of dust. The dog and I went to the outfield, where I hurled the ball as far as I could for him to chase. Each time he brought it back and dropped it at my feet, panting, showing his teeth in what I was pretty sure was a smile. After a while I felt a chill and we went back inside.

Corrections and Clarifications

The caption for the photo of yesterday's city council meeting (Section 1, Page 2) misidentified Lawrence Billings as Horance Willings. We regret the error.

In Wednesday's lead editorial, we declared that Sheriff Jack Seager is an ineffectual public servant whose slipshod leadership is plunging our town into a death spiral of crime and corruption. We regret this because we actually think, as sheriffs go, he's doing a pretty good job. And when you mention the words "crime" and "this town" together people generally laugh and say, "What crime?" and "Where?" What we meant to say is word has it that Sheriff Seager has a really small dick.

Now that we think about it, we also regret that we were unable to hit the ball to the right side in order to move the runner from first into scoring position during the big state playoff game all those years ago.

That time we said we would set the TiVo for your favorite show and it must've recorded the wrong channel, or the time was messed up or something? We regret that.

The thing is, we thought that Horance Willings was an awfully strange name, but frankly, we were quite taken with it. Still and all, we regret the error.

Speaking of high school, we regret staring at Julie Norman's chest.

We also shouldn't let the recyclables pile up like that in the corner of the kitchen. It's kind of messy and attracts bugs. We regret this.

We regret that during the undressing period of our noontime coupling with Mrs. Seager, consumed as we were by our furtive passion, we flung our underpants *all the way under* the clothes dresser, which made them very hard to find when Sheriff Seager unexpectedly came home for lunch.

Remember Lawrence Billings? Turns out he prefers Larry. We should have asked. It smarts when you compound one error with another. It really does. We regret this.

Actually, what we regret is *getting caught* staring at Julie Norman's chest. It made us look like a pervert.

We have some very small regrets over failing to read the assembly directions for that prefabricated bookshelf.

We regret also that we spent so much time searching for the underwear, rushing around the Seager bedroom in the altogether. We should have ditched them and gone commando. Precious moments were lost there for sure. Regrets.

In our defense, we are right-handed and were given nothing but hard cheese on the inner half of the plate. Nevertheless, regrets are ours.

Failure to recycle belies a kind of careless attitude toward the larger needs of the community. We wish we could get it together on this front.

Shoving our foot through the fly of our boxers once the boxers were finally located was also a problem.

What we mean is that we regret that first we referred to Larry Billings as Horance Willings, then compounded the error by calling him "Lawrence" when it is now clear that only his mother calls him "Lawrence." We don't regret that his name is Larry or that making errors leads to regrets. Errors should have consequences, and while we count ourselves lucky when consequences don't result from our errors, we accept them when they do.

That guy was all-conference. First team. Veins ran down his forearm. If we were supposed to bunt, we would have bunted, but the signs were to swing away with an eye toward hitting to the right side. If there's a regret, it's that we didn't back out of the batter's box, call time, and clarify things with the third-base coach, stressing our doubts about our ability to get good wood on this guy's stuff.

We've never told our father we loved him, never felt the rasp of his whiskers on our lips. We regret this.

We're grateful for Mrs. Julie Seager's laughter as we searched for the underwear. Given the inherent franticness and tension of the situation, that she sat up in the bed with the sheet only half-covering her breasts and held her hand over her mouth as she did the aforementioned laughing really seemed to take the edge off, despite the heavy tread of her husband's, Sheriff Seager's, trooper boots on the stairs.

Regarding the bookshelf, we agree that the side with the faux-woodgrain contact paper looks better on the outside than does the one with the plain medium-density fiberboard. On the other hand, we *do not* regret *not* disassembling then reassembling the bookshelf all over again because we feel that the bookshelf looks just fine, or at least as fine as a prefabricated, medium-density fiberboard bookshelf can look, as long as the offending, non-faux-woodgrain side is pushed against the wall, which it is.

Oh, how she filled out that sweater!

We mean it's not our fault; you know that TiVo has always been a little screwy. Gets things wrong all the time it does.

There's no shame in calling time, jogging down the foul line, and discussing options. There's no hurry. It's baseball. So why didn't we do it? Arrrrggggghhhhh!

As it turns out, Larry Billings's mother is deceased, so where we indicated that "only his mother *calls* him Lawrence" we should have said *called*. We deeply regret the error. In fact, we owe you one, Lar.

We don't regret keeping our mouth shut over the postgame getting-stuffed-into-the-locker incident. We are no stoolie.

We're thankful to the Hauer gun company for the tendency of their HP-9 model to jam when fired from a nonlevel position. We imagine that in retrospect, despite the yelling and the banging of the gun first on the standing lamp, then on the dresser, then lamp, and finally the fleshy spot where our neck meets our shoulder, Sheriff Seager is thankful as well, since the actual firing of a gun at another person, especially an unarmed one without any clothes on, almost always leads to serious, nearly permanent regrets. You'd have to ask him about that, though.

There is a certain precise ballet to the double play. Because of this, they are rare in high school ball. Nevertheless, we regret not running our feeble grounder out harder. We said this over and over at the time. Sorry sorry sorry, please don't. Ouch ouch. Sorry sorry sorry, so sorry. Ouch.

Sometimes we have regrets over finding and realizing love late in life, but these regrets are eased by love's presence.

Apparently it's always "Larry," never "Lar." This won't happen again, we swear. Let us buy you a beer.

Truthfully, we were a little surprised that we made contact at all, so it wasn't a failure to run hard, but the split-second (or slightly longer than split-second) hesitation that killed us. Once we started running, it was really as fast as we could manage.

That the realization of this love has come at the expense of another man causes barely noticeable regrets.

We're conflicted about our father's tears on that night after we failed to move the runner over and were stuffed in the locker.

Did the Hauer gun company have to make the butt of the HP-9 model so hard and kind of pointy? We regret they decided to do that for sure. Our shoulder feels like it's going to hurt for some time. Do you hear that, the clicking noise when it's raised? There it is again. Do you think it's a tendon?

We still do regret that we couldn't run faster.

We double-checked it, time, date, everything. We looked the date up on the calendar and the channel in the on-screen guide. We were very thorough and careful because we knew it was important.

If we'd really been thinking, rather than screaming and pounding at the inside of the locker door, knowing full well that the teammates who stripped us naked, black-markered "Loser" on our forehead, and shut us in the locker in the first place were not going to let us out, we would have tried some deep, centering breaths, in order to get as comfortable as possible while waiting for morning's custodial crew.

We lied about having "barely noticeable" regrets over our love coming at the expense of another man. Truth is, we have no regrets at all. None.

We regret offering to buy Larry Billings, who is, we've come to find out, a recovering alcoholic, a beer.

None.

You see, the thing about this prefabricated furniture is that the predrilled holes for the premeasured screws never quite line up, which means you really have to torque those things in there in order to get it all assembled, only to realize that the faux-woodgrain contact-paper side is facing the wrong way is really frustrating, and after a couple of hours of sweat getting the thing so it at least stands up mostly level and unwobbly, thinking about starting over again makes us want to cry, which is something we haven't done in quite a few years.

Words of praise go out to the makers of the Megaflex progressive resistance muscle training system. No regrets about that purchase, no sirs!

Julie Norman releasing us from the locker imprisonment was a mixed blessing to be sure. On the plus side, we did not have to wait for the custodial crew, and just after we tumbled from the locker, there was the brief clutching to her sweater-covered chest, the smell of fall and pencil erasers. But there was also her sad eyes on our cold, fish-belly skin. That was hard to take.

While we're glad that Sheriff Seager "must've slipped on the rug" (as he claims) after landing the initial shoulder blow with the Hauer HP-9, we think it's more likely that our work with the Megaflex had something to do with it. Nonetheless, we're also grateful that the state has some really low fitness-recheck requirements for its law enforcement officers.

On the other hand, we suspect, and have suspected for some time, that "recyclables" get dumped into the same trash pile as everything else, which would make the concept of recycling pretty much moot.

We admit that we weren't thinking of this originally, but perhaps Larry Billings would be interested in a nonalcoholic beer. We had an uncle once who had his trouble with the ale and spirits, but he would drink the nonalcoholic beer. We'd like to do something to soothe our regrets.

We regret that the school administration stocked the locker-room shower with the liquid, nonfoaming, antibacterial soap. It does not work for scrubbing off marker, nor does it leave one smelling or feeling fresh after a couple hours inside a gym locker. It leaves one smelling like the bottom of a chemistry-lab sink.

We have slight qualms about digging our knee so hard into Sheriff Seager's back as Mrs. Julie Seager née Norman lashed his hands and feet with lamp cord, allowing us to retrieve our clothes and run to the Sundowner Motor Lodge, Route 14, just past the public access and before the spot where the old oak fell during that microburst last summer.

At the time, we were certain that our father's tears were over our failure at the plate, or our pathetic appearance: wrapped in towels, feet black from the barefoot walk home, forehead scrubbed raw to near bleeding. We thought (foolishly) that he was ashamed.

We shouldn't have lied about that TiVo thing earlier. The truth is we forgot, or actually we remembered ten minutes into the show, which we thought would look bad considering our rock-solid promise to do this one thing, so we made up that other story, which actually worked, we think, which leads us to believe we might come to regret this little confession.

We think now that our father meant to comfort us, that he was waiting for us, and as he was waiting, the tears just got the better of him. We should have known this all along, but regret the self-absorption of youth that leads one to think the whole world is aligned against them. In our defense, it had been a very bad evening. We had reason to believe the worst about people.

We are grateful for the chalky mints in the dented tin dish at the front desk of the Sundowner Motor Lodge because we left without toothbrushes and all the stores were closed, and fresh breath was important at the time.

What is clear is that the sort of people who buy prefabricated furniture (which we are) are the kind of people unlikely to be bothered by imperfect assembly.

Regarding the Larry situation, we've known guys who'll fall off the wagon just smelling a beer, and if Larry's one of those guys, then even a nonalcoholic beer is probably a bad idea.

That small-dick crack regarding Sheriff Seager was unfair. We take it back, despite its obvious truth. Of course, it's easy to be charitable when one has secured the ultimate victory and said victory involves long sessions of lovemaking with a girl you've loved since you first saw her sweater.

How do we know this about our father, then? Have we discussed that evening? No. Let us say this, though: He lives alone now. He makes model ships inside bottles. He uses strands saved from our mother's hair to lash the tiny sailcloth to the miniature mast. We think this means something.

We're thankful for video on demand and their ameliorative effects on people who miss pivotal episodes of their favorite family dramas due to TiVo failures.

If we were to outlive her, which we doubt will happen, but if so, we think we may be like our father and use something of her to make something else. But her hair falls in long curls, not straight like our mother's. We'd have to think of something different.

In truth, the recyclables winding up with the piles of nonrecyclable trash doesn't really bother us all that much. At this moment, to us, it appears that everything is abundant.

Not Schmitty

Here we are in the house weight room, though it is not really the weight room because it is the boiler room, the place where the boiler is, the boiler that heats the house we live in together as brothers.

It is an old house. And at night, in the cold months, the boiler clangs and clanks, which tells us that it is working at least.

It is a fraternity house, not a frat house. Do you call your mother a "mutt?" Your country a . . . you get the idea.

Everyone who has ever lived in the house, living or dead, is a brother. This is how it has worked, always.

The boiler room is where we also decided to lift weights because there was room for benches and barbells and it's important to exercise so we look good. We don't say virile because if we said that word it would sound gay, but that's essentially what's going on. We have an image to maintain, after all, a good one. Masculine virtue, emphasis on the masculine. When you say our letters there are associations, positive ones, and there's a certain duty to nurture what our other brothers before us have built.

Schmitty is the obvious choice for what we have planned, the reason we are in the weight room/boiler room. And what we have planned is to waterboard Schmitty.

We can't remember whose idea it was. Inside the house we are either alone or in packs of three or more, never two, because if two of us are seen coming out of a room together, we will say something like, *What were you two faggots up to in there?*

We always laugh at that. To react otherwise means we were definitely up to some faggoty shit, because why would we be so pissed if we weren't 69-ing each other like a couple of complete homos? Which is to say we were in a group of at least three and more likely five or more when we said, *You know what we should do? We should do that waterboarding shit. To the pledges.*

And then, after a couple seconds' thought, we replied, *That really would be badass, waterboarding our pledges.*

We shared a chorus of *yeah* and *totally,* and we took out our phones and googled waterboarding videos, and as we watched them we realized that this idea was even better than first thought because that shit is really badass. We wouldn't even need to have rush anymore because waterboarding sells itself. Everyone will know that we are the fraternity so badass that people are willing to be waterboarded to belong.

That is so fucked up, we said. *And also fuckingtabulously badass.*

We knew that someone had to try it first, to make sure we knew how to do it, because experience tells us the quickest way to shut down a chapter is to kill a pledge.

We decided on Schmitty, who is just now complaining a little about the ropes lashing him to the decline weight bench being too tight. We decided on Schmitty because Schmitty is tough, and also loves the house. Schmitty already has our letters branded on his ass, which is cool, not faggoty, even though all of us were staring at Schmitty's naked, rather muscular butt when it happened.

The branding was way badass. It was the kind of thing we talked about doing all the time, but Schmitty was the only one who agreed to it, and not only did Schmitty go through with it, but even as a couple of us blew chunks at the smell of Schmitty's ass flesh burning, Schmitty just growled like a motherfucking animal until it was done, and sometimes during chapter meetings—which are secret, so we're not supposed to tell this—when we say something that Schmitty agrees with, he drops his pants and flashes the brand and the debate is ended.

Schmitty was the obvious choice for those reasons, and also because he was already in the weight room on the very decline bench to which he is now strapped. The bench is in the decline position in order for Schmitty to work the lower portion of his pectoral muscles, and also because when you waterboard someone you place a cloth over their nose and mouth and then pour water over them to simulate drowning, and if you don't place them in a decline position, the water does not run over the nostrils in sufficient volume to simulate drowning.

This is what we emphasize to Schmitty, that the drowning is simulated, not actual, because he's starting to alternate between looking anxious and angry, pulling harder and harder on the ropes as we drape an old gym towel over his face. *We're not really going to kill you, dumbass,* we say. We're pretty sure Schmitty agreed to this, but in the end it doesn't matter, because we've decided that this is what needs doing.

There is very little light in the weight/boiler room, just a sixty-watt bulb dangling from a single fixture. The sweat on Schmitty's pectorals shines in this light. Schmitty can bench 305 for 12 reps, which is impressive. The floor is concrete slab with long cracks running through it, some of them patched. Schmitty is trying to blow the towel off his face, thrashing his head around, but we remedy this by grabbing the towel ends and pinning Schmitty's head to the bench. The tendons in his neck flex memorably.

It is hot in the boiler room because it is the boiler room. Generations of water stains that look like Rorschach blots mar the brick walls.

We only have enough rope to tie Schmitty's arms, so we decide to sit on his legs, which had been thrashing around like he is treading water, which we recognize is not an example of irony.

Schmitty is making noises underneath the towel.

Is that crying? we ask, and then decide no way because Schmitty would not cry.

We ask ourselves *How much water?* We shrug because we figure that Schmitty's reaction will tell us how much is enough, and how much is too much.

It's important to note that in this moment, we love Schmitty. We love each other. We love ourselves, but most of all we love Schmitty because he is one of us. We are brothers, all. We would never do anything to hurt Schmitty because that would be like cutting off our own legs. In fact, we maybe have never loved each other more. That we are waterboarding Schmitty is the proof.

Under the cloth held over his face, Schmitty gags and retches. We pour the water in intervals, five seconds on, five seconds off. This, says the Internet, is how it must be done to avoid consequences like the subject being waterboarded passing out, which defeats the purpose of waterboarding them. Soon, Schmitty stops trying to kick us off his legs and no longer pulls at the ropes. He's only gurgling now. His limbs are slack. The towel, taut over his face, is sucked into his mouth with his breath. His wrists are raw. They may scar, but no worse than a brand, for sure.

We waterboard Schmitty until it is no longer interesting to waterboard Schmitty, until we know what there is to know about waterboarding, which is astoundingly simple and doesn't take all that much time, it turns out. We remove the towel from Schmitty's face, and for a moment we worry that maybe we did it wrong, that we killed Schmitty, because his eyes are—how can we put this?—absent. They are open, but no one is present, like this is a life-sized Schmitty doll in front of us, eyes black and staring and lifeless, except we know Schmitty is not dead because his chest rises and falls.

We say his name, *Schmitty! Schmitty!* We slap his cheeks and say his name, *Schmitty! Schmitty!* Some of us in the back giggle nervously. *Holy fuck,* we say.

And then Schmitty returns, except that clearly it is Not Schmitty. It is Schmitty's body and Schmitty's face, but we know it is Not Schmitty because Not Schmitty raises his head up and looks us in the eyes and says: *You motherfuckers better leave me tied up because if I ever get loose I'm going to kill every single one of you.*

Schmitty would never say that.

We do the smart thing, the only thing, and leave Not Schmitty in the boiler room, lashed to the bench. We turn off the lights and shut the door and we go upstairs to our rooms; we brace a chair under the knob and we listen hard for the approach of Not Schmitty, because we're assuming that like Schmitty, Not Schmitty can also bench 305 pounds for 12 reps, and unlike Schmitty, Not Schmitty has vowed to kill every one of us.

We sit upright in our beds and consider how Not Schmitty might kill us. Bare hands is an option, Not Schmitty gripping our throats, squeezing. Or the ropes we used to tether him to the decline weight bench wound around our necks until our heads practically pop off our bodies. That's a possibility. Not Schmitty could knock on our doors, and when we answer, he could bring a twenty-five-pound barbell down on our heads. He could get one of the large butcher's knives from the kitchen and he could slip up behind us and ram the blade between our ribs into an organ like the spleen that will let loose our blood inside our bodies until there is not enough blood left for our hearts to continue pumping.

We have one sleepless night, then another. When the boiler kicks in we listen for the clanks and clangs in the radiators and wonder if there is a rhythm to them, if Not Schmitty is tapping out a message of our dooms. We stop thinking about Not Schmitty so we can think more about ourselves, our vulnerable selves.

Eventually, life has to go on. We emerge from our rooms, blinking, seeing everything as it was, and we wonder if maybe it was a dream, if maybe we never decided to waterboard Schmitty, and therefore there is no Not Schmitty still tied to the decline bench in the weight/boiler room.

We do not go to look for ourselves, no. We put up plastic sheeting in front of the stairwell, and a sign warning of asbestos.

We do not go to look because it is easier to move forward rather than to examine the past, if indeed the past even happened. We miss Schmitty for sure, but Schmitty remains in our hearts, so it is not like Schmitty is entirely gone. Remember that time Schmitty bet us he could gain twenty pounds in a day and he ate and ate and ate, spaghetti and stir-fry and chocolate pudding, and he actually did it, and we said, *How about that fucking Schmitty?*

Of course we remember.

But we move on. We go to class. We party. We go to more class. We wear shirts with the collars popped and boat shoes even though we don't have boats, yet. We party. We graduate. We party. We get jobs. We start lives in apartments. We go to work. We participate in March Madness pools. We meet girls, whom we know enough to call women to their faces. We fall in love. We deny falling in love because being in love is kind of gay, even if it's with a girl (woman). We know we are in love because when we say disgusting things about our girlfriends to our brothers, we feel regret. We go to work. We save money for a ring. We go to work. We propose. We have weddings at which we deny crying during the ceremony, after which we get shitty via open bars.

We have families. We buy homes. We buy homes and have families of tiny, vulnerable children who grow into small, vulnerable children, and then slightly less small, but still vulnerable children. With the children, we fear Not Schmitty is everywhere, for example driving the car in front of us, waiting for an opportunity to stop short, causing us to rear-end him, which will launch our small, vulnerable children in their improperly secured car seats through the windshield.

Not Schmitty could be anywhere. When we are in the office bathroom, solo in a stall taking a dump, and the bathroom door swings open and we hear footsteps, we think of Not Schmitty and his doll's eyes and we wait for a shotgun blast through the stall door that will splatter us across the tile.

After we make love to the girl (woman) we love and fall asleep— because the lovemaking is like a very strenuous sport—we awake with a start, thrashing our arms, certain Not Schmitty has come with a pillow meant for our faces. Even as we draw back our titanium driver, ready to send a laser down the fairway, we are certain that Not Schmitty is behind us with a nine iron, waiting to cave in our skulls.

We miss the days we lived with our brothers, when we were young and strong and not vulnerable, but invulnerable.

We grow older. We buy boats. We buy boats we don't use all that often, and we complain that boats are just bottomless holes you pour money into, which tells people that we not only own boats, but also have wealth enough not to worry about pouring money into them.

Our guts grow past our ability to suck them in. Our bench press maxes drop toward the double digits. The more money we make, the less work we seem to do. Sixty-five percent of us vote Republican; the rest of us must be gay or poor or something. Recessions happen in which we're barely touched. We see our children graduate high school and then college, things they achieve despite our suspicion that some of them are dumb or defective, though we love them anyway, which is an astounding thing. Our wives spread in places we wish they wouldn't. We achieve all the trappings of success. We are helpful to each other in innumerable ways at this, business referrals, stock tips, sales leads, stock tips, football tickets, stock tips. This is what we were promised so many years ago by the brotherhood, and it has come true.

When the kids leave the house for good we go to Europe.

Why Europe? We don't know. It's just something we're supposed to do. Some people it is Disneyland, others go to all-inclusive resorts in the Bahamas, we are supposed to go to Europe. It is as though we are trapped by this need, even though we have limited desire to go to Europe and are even a little afraid to go to Europe, the language barrier and all. When we go to Europe, in Europe in those European eyes we become what we know ourselves to be: rich, tacky, successful, fat.

We have the trips of our lives, obviously, but are nonetheless happy to come home. It is evening, and the motion sensor snaps the light on as we approach, which always makes us freeze for a moment, like we are stealing our own luggage. There are ten steps from the flagstone walk to the portico, so that the house may loom over the yard, making its statement. Once inside, we have that sensation that someone has been here in our absence. The air-conditioning is too high. We smell popcorn. We whistle for the dog and then remember he is at the kennel until morning. Our wives go upstairs for a bath and we consider the possibility of joining them, something done in the past, but that past is awfully distant, and there is the matter of logistics in terms of fitting inside the tub, and so we discard the notion and feel sad that we can't figure out how to make it work.

We drink a whisky. It is expensive and bitter. The house is large, so our bathing wives can't even be heard. These are the times when we listen to the creak of the wood floors for Not Schmitty's approach. We hold ourselves upright, hands pressed to the kitchen granite and refuse to turn around. Perhaps Not Schmitty has already made short work of our wives, their blood pinking the bath mat, which is what we would do if we were Not Schmitty, if we wanted to deliver maximum hurt. Once we picture our wives' blood swirling through the bath water we can't stop this vision, but we resist rushing upstairs because what if Not Schmitty is there, waiting? What if he is waiting, holding an ax with a chip in the blade from use?

What if he holds an ax above his head, an ax that glints in the blue light through the parted curtains and he will use it to smite us in two and there's nothing we can do about it?

But he's not here, is he?

Is he?

Second Careers

I don't think that Christ would be shy to shake off his gloves and protect his teammates.
— STU GRIMSON, NHL enforcer/born-again Christian

Jesus? Jesus Christ? Yeah, sure I remember him, a scrapper, a real character guy. I mean, Jesus Christ, he was Jesus Christ, you know?
— BOB MORRISON, Jesus's Coach with the Saskatoon Bear Trap of the Near Western Outpost Hockey League (NWOHL)

He'd go to war for you for sure, always there to defend a guy, but once, when Scialabba pole-axed him, just clubbed the living shit out of Jesus right between the shoulder blades, Jesus didn't do anything, that SOB just turned the other cheek. "Vengeance be not man's but God's," he said . . . Course we couldn't take any chances, so next shift, I got Scialabba with a nice hearty jab in the stones, if you know what I'm saying.
— VINCENT DALMPIERRE, Jesus's former Bear Trap teammate

Yeah, Jesus always wanted to score more—who didn't? But he knew that wasn't his role. He used to say, "I know, I know, smite the wicked, dispatch the base." He never enjoyed it like the real psychos did, though. He didn't *relish* the job like some of them, like that freak Scialabba. I mean, you could tell it wore on Jesus sometimes, like he had the weight of the world on his shoulders.
— RANDY DUCHESNE, Jesus's former Bear Trap teammate

Jesus always was a great one for stories, like on those awful bus trips between Hamilton and Saskatoon; you could always count on him to pass the time. He had this one about the traveling salesman, the milk-maid, and the fig tree. I never did figure out what the hell he meant, but oh man, that one always busted my gut.

    —CLAUDE LALONDE, Jesus's former Bear Trap teammate

Jesus was a cheap-shot, chickenshit life-ruining motherfucker.

    —RICH SCIALABBA, former player, Hamilton Force

It's not that he couldn't score; I saw him do some amazing things sometimes, some real miracles with the puck, and he always had the good, hard slapper, but remember, we had guys like Conrad and Lan-glois on that team, so someone had to do the mucking in the corners. When the shit is heavy and you've gotta hack your way out of the jungle, you need a machete. Our machete was Jesus.

    —DALMPIERRE

Never did care for the guy. Tough little player, but every time I called a penalty on him it was always, "Judge not lest ye be judged," and I'd be like, "What the hell does that mean?" And well, yeah, there was that thing with Scialabba, that wasn't too good. I saw the whole thing . . . not a memory I care for, for sure.

    —CONRAD GAULTHIER, referee, Near Western Outpost
      Hockey League

I'm not going to say he didn't have it coming, but you hate to see that kind of thing happen, even to a prick like Scialabba.

    —DUCHESNE

Sure, I took some heat. They said I sent Jesus out there just to mess up Scialabba, but let me get a few things straight. First, this is hockey, not goddamn tiddlywinks. Second, Scialabba had been taking liberties all series and had to be stopped; the faint of heart don't win the Richards Cup. Lastly, I didn't have to say anything about what to do with Scialabba, not word one to Jesus. He knew what had to be done because he was all about what was good for the team.

—MORRISON

No, I didn't see it. I'm glad I didn't. Who wants that memory?

—LALONDE

I'll tell you something about Jesus, what he was like as a player. Afterward, after the thing with Scialabba, Jesus went back into the locker room and wept. Jesus wept.

—DUCHESNE

You might call it a moment of truth, you could call it that, and yeah, maybe in that moment I felt some fear. You've got Jesus coming at you with a hockey stick, and you'd be a little afraid, wouldn't you?

—SCIALABBA

I saw most of it. Scialabba had just planted Scully into the boards from behind, after the whistle, messed Scully up pretty bad, and so Jesus went after him. I mean, that's what he was supposed to do.

—DUCHESNE

It was a lot of blood. The screams were tough. It even almost made me feel bad for Scialabba, but that miserable fuck had to be dealt with. It's part of the game.

—DALMPIERRE

I'm just thankful that Janice was at home with the kids.

—SCIALABBA

Jesus just kept saying "An eye for an eye, an eye for an eye." To his credit, Scialabba didn't run, but he was plenty scared all right, anyone could see that.

—GAULTHIER

The incision was really quite clean, extending several centimeters along the orbital ridge and ending just above the maxillary. There wasn't much left for us to do but fit Mr. Scialabba for the prosthetic.

—DR. PAUL DUFRESNE, Chief of Retinal Surgery,
Blessed Heart of St. Mary Hospital

The suspension was for life, all leagues, organized hockey, period. I didn't want to see him in the Moose Jaw over-35 no-check Wednesday-night church league. Mr. Christ had to find another line of work.

—JEAN-PIERRE VALMONT, Commissioner NWOHL

Nights are toughest. It's a dry cold up here, and that makes the socket ache. The painkillers stopped working years ago, and Rich Scialabba is not going to be some kind of dope fiend.

—SCIALABBA

I know it hurts him some when I have to clean the socket. He's not careful enough about it, so it's up to me to take the swab and some alcohol and work around the edges. It's all pretty healed, but I know it still stings sometimes. Instead of wincing, though, he smiles at me. That's how I know when it hurts him, when he smiles. It's like when we first started dating and Rich was working his way up through the minors and he had to do a lot of fighting. He would come over after a game, his hair wet and slicked back from a shower, always wearing a tie. I would wait for him, watching through a part in the curtains. Sometimes he limped a little, and sometimes I could see a fresh shiner under his eye as he passed under a streetlight and came up the drive.

Most days he'd ring the doorbell with his elbow because his hands were so sore. For a long time he insisted on shaking my father's hand when it was held out to him, until I told Daddy to stop doing that because of how much it hurt Rich. After that, Daddy just sort of waved, and Rich would do the same and then stand and talk to my father, hiding his hands clasped behind his back.

    —JANICE SCIALABBA

People think I should be bitter, but I try to be thankful for some things; it doesn't pay not to be. The settlement left us comfortable, and Janice and the kids are great. I miss the game, sure I do, but the game doesn't define who you are unless you let it. I think that's what happened to Jesus. He just let it get too far into him. You do a job for your team, but that's all it is. My job was to fight, his too. I loved the game, still do, but you can't let it be your religion. I've got other things . . . like for instance, days with Janice and Richie and Meagan are mostly long and slow and good here. Meagan says she's going to be a dancer, ballet. I don't know where she gets that, but sometimes she begs me to be her partner, and I do it to make her happy. I cradle her across the room like I'm some kind of Baryshnikov. Meg stretches out her arms and points her toes and keeps a super-serious look on her face. It's funny, but she likes to perform dying scenes the most. She hugs herself as she folds to the floor, very graceful, very beautiful. She has long fingers, from her mother. Most afternoons, I head out to the ponds to skate with little Richie. He's good, fast like I never was, nice touch with the stick. He's only eight, but still, when he really gets moving his coat cracks behind him in the wind like some sort of cape. I can only skate in circles now. I chase after him making one long left turn. My arm waves around for balance and I know I look like some kind of clown. As he skates away, Richie sometimes looks over his shoulder and laughs at me, but not in a bad way.

    —SCIALABBA

Homosexuals Threaten the Sanctity of Norman's Marriage

They started in on a Tuesday, late fall. It was morning, and as Norman took the garbage to the curb, he could see them loosely huddled near the bagged leaves that waited for pickup. Damn it, he thought. Homosexuals in the yard.

They'd come to threaten the sanctity of his marriage, but Norman wasn't having it.

"Morning," he said. Norman tries to be friendly to everybody regardless. That's how he was raised. American values.

"Good morning," they replied. A couple of them wore nicely tailored suits that looked just a bit snug in the seat. One had a lime-green sweater tied around his neck. Their grooming was impeccable. Another had a perfectly straight trail of hair plunging down his chest, accentuated by the open front of his shirt. Still another was clad entirely in leather; he squeaked whenever he moved. A few looked just about like anyone else. To Norman, they all smelled citrusy. Norman turned to make his way back to the house.

"You don't show her the proper attention," one of them called after him.

"Excuse me?"

"Your wife; you take her for granted," another said.

"I love my wife."

They looked at each other and smiled. "Of course you do." The man with the lime-green sweater slipped his arm around the waist of one that looked just about like anyone else. "But when's the last time you *really* looked at her?" he asked. The other man turned to face the man with the sweater. They closed their eyes and brought their faces close together, brushing noses.

Norman didn't need to see that stuff. He went back inside.

Ellie was moving around the kitchen. Those fellows didn't know what they were talking about. Norman looked at his wife every day. Norman watched as she took the breakfast plates from the table to the sink. Her bottom shook underneath her robe as she scrubbed the plates. Her hair medium-length and brown. The ankles thicker than you'd think, but not in a bad way. Norman had been looking at her for years. How many years? Thirty-six. What was left to see?

Norman stood to leave for work. He wondered if he should say something to Ellie about the homosexuals outside, or if it would just cause her worry. Ellie placed the dishes in the washer. Norman cleared his throat as if to speak and Ellie smiled, waving the scrub brush in farewell. Saying nothing, Norman walked out of the kitchen, to the garage, to the car. He backed out of the driveway without looking, wondering if he might feel a bump as he ran over the whole pack of them.

Norman didn't see them for a while after that first encounter, but then one evening, as he went to retrieve the recycling bin, there they were, playing hopscotch along the sidewalk. There seemed to be more this time. They clapped loudly for each other as they went for each successive square. Norman thought, but didn't say, *Fairies*.

"We've been meaning to tell you," the one with the lime-green sweater said, dribbling his stone into a hopscotch square, "your moves in the bedroom, they're limited."

"What do you mean?"

"For one thing, are you always on top?" he asked, hopping toward his stone.

"Is there another way?"

"Would you like us to demonstrate?" He paused and looked at Norman.

"Lord no."

"We could show you some things." The one in the lime-green sweater held his hands outstretched at his waist and pumped his hips forward.

"No, please, no."

"Homophobic?"

"Midwestern."

They laughed. Norman did a little as well. He knew deep down he wasn't homophobic. He was pretty positive he'd known some gays, treated them well, treated them just like anyone else. He didn't hate people for what they were or for what they chose to be. That wasn't Norman's way.

The one with the lime-green sweater tied around his neck stood on one foot and bent to retrieve his stone, his arm stretched down, his leg levering into the air from his hip.

"Anytime, though, if you want," he said, skipping back to safety.

Not always on top. Mostly, but not every time, Norman thought. Ellie had been his only and his always, and that should mean something. They were getting older for sure, but they were not dormant, no sirs. Some nights, they would be watching television side by side on the couch and their knees would touch and there would be a little twitch up Norman's leg, an ache that climbs to you know where, and it is the same ache as when she first let him kiss her under the bleachers back in high school, when they went outside to steal a smoke and Norman leaned into her, as though drawn by a magnet, pressing his lips harder against hers until she ducked away and he clanged his head against one of the support bars.

Those nights, once in bed, Norman will slide her nightgown up and run the back of his nail along her thigh, and that is his sign. Hers is a change in her breathing, deeper, longer, and when she is ready she will slip out from underneath her nightgown and Norman will shed his bottoms and climb on top, bracing himself so as not to crush her, and there they are. One man and one woman, together. As it was in the Garden, as it has been since, and as it should be forever.

They were back again a few weeks later. It had snowed, and Norman was out shoveling the drive. They wore puffy winter coats with fur-trimmed hoods, except for the leather-clad one who still wore his leather, now accentuated with matching gloves, and the average ones who wore long overcoats. As Norman cleared the snow, they frolicked in the yard, making snow angels and flinging snowballs at each other. Frankly, Norman thought, they threw like girls.

The one with the lime-green sweater ran up to Norman. He clutched a fistful of snow, cocking his arm back, free arm pointed toward Norman as the target.

"Please don't," Norman said.

He dropped the snow to the ground and brushed his hands to-gether. "I wouldn't," he said. Norman scraped another strip of the drive clean, piled the snow into berms along the sides.

"So," he said.

"What?"

"Gina," he said. He stretched the name out (Geeee-nahhh) and smiled and looked up at Norman from under his hood. He wiggled his eyebrows.

"What does that mean?"

"Gina," he said, "from work. You watch her. She *is* hot. Even we can see that. We may be gay, but we're not dead."

Gina. She had some skirts, no doubt about it; Norman was not dead either. Her mode of dress was not really appropriate for the workplace, but Norman had not made a careful study of her wardrobe or anything. He'd always been faithful to Ellie, and ogling women was rude. "I don't know what you're talking about," he said.

"Hawwwww," he laughed, tilting his head back. "That wasn't your wife you were thinking about bending over the copier and tugging her panties down as your trousers dropped to your ankles. I'm pretty sure of that."

So this was their game, Norman thought; sow doubt, undermine traditions with their free-love hedonism. He wasn't going to have any of it. He'd thought no such things. Norman raised the shovel over his head. "Back off!"

"Whoa, big guy," he said, raising his hands and retreating. "Don't kill the messenger, my man. We're not here to harm." He turned and jogged back to his companions and rejoined the hijinks. Norman quickly finished the driveway and retreated inside.

Gina. Was it possible that she began to linger overlong at Norman's desk? She is younger, but not so much younger. Twelve years? Fifteen? Twenty? She is lean, and her walk is strong. She smiles at him often, but then Norman is her boss and this is not a bad strategy with a boss. Norman knows that gender dynamics have changed over the years and that successful women sometimes use their womanness to their advantage. Her skirts stretch very tightly over her hips and they ride up high. Norman does not remember this style of skirt on the young women of his generation. In high school, the boys would duck their heads to peek at the girls' calves beneath their hemlines, and that's what he first saw of Ellie. The ankles a bit thick, yes, but the calves, shapely, promising something interesting higher on the leg. With the skirts today, no imagining is necessary, but in seeing them, the mind races, Norman thinks, and not in a good way. And the breasts, they tremble above the open neck of her blouse; a small charm tumbles down the gap from a necklace, inviting one to look. On cold winter days, she entered the office hugged by a heavy coat, covered, but then she shook free from the coat and there she was, all of her, the skirt, the blouse.

These newer styles seemed wrong, inappropriate, but . . . effective, was the word that came to Norman's mind.

They started showing up at work, one or two of them in the bathroom or the kitchenette. Norman wondered how they got past security. Everyone in the building was supposed to wear a name badge. "So," the one with the lime-green sweater said, "dinner with Gina."

"It's with the whole team," Norman replied, stirring powdered creamer into his coffee. "Thanks for a job well done."

The man frowned at Norman's cup. "How do you drink that crap?" he said. "Ever hear of a mochaccino?"

"I've been drinking it every day, and no, I wouldn't know about mochaccinos."

The man went to the fridge and pawed through the leftover lunches, grimacing at the Chinese takeout containers and a half-eaten Caesar salad with breaded chicken strips. "Ugh, you people are going to eat yourselves into your graves. Want to see my six-pack?"

"Is there something you wanted?" Norman said, sighing.

He shut the fridge and turned to Norman. "You drink that sludge every day, and I'm sure you think it suits you just fine, but the truth is I've seen you drive by the coffee places and you're curious about the lattes, the mochaccinos, the frappuccinos."

"I don't even know what those are, nor do I care," Norman said. Truthfully, Norman often found himself staring at the windows of these coffee places that suddenly seemed everywhere, wondering about the possibilities inside, but he would never go in for fear of making himself the fool by ordering wrongly. "Why break what doesn't need fixing?" Norman said.

Norman thought the man looked at him with something like pity, but it should've been the other way around given his situation, his status. "If you say so," the man said, flouncing out of the kitchenette and into the hallway.

* * *

"I won't be home for dinner tomorrow night," Norman said to Ellie as they sat down to eat that evening. Wednesday, which meant meatloaf, which Norman enjoyed with generous mounds of ketchup.

"No?"

"I'm taking the whole team out to celebrate. We're up 22 percent this year over last." Norman shook the ketchup bottle vigorously, mixing the contents, making sure he wasn't stuck with a runny initial burst out of the squeeze top.

"No spouses?"

"They're all single, dearest. Besides, it isn't in the budget."

"Even though you're up 22 percent?"

Norman could not tell whether Ellie was teasing him. Her face was bent over her plate as she shoveled a forkful of green beans into her mouth.

Norman got a little huffy. "We're the only ones up more than single digits. Some groups are even down." He crammed a bite of meatloaf into his mouth and chewed roughly. Looking up, he could see two or three of the homosexuals outside the window over Ellie's shoulder, waving at him like small children. Norman frowned.

"That's wonderful, dear," Ellie said. "I just wish I could be in on the celebration is all. I'm proud of you." Her voice trailed off near the end, becoming barely audible, but Norman made no notice because he was distracted by the antics of the homosexuals. One of the suit-wearing ones donned a long dark wig and hung a sign around his neck with "Gina" on it in bold letters. The lime-green-sweatered one came up from behind and groped the other man's chest while thrusting his pelvis against his backside. Norman tried to wave them off without Ellie seeing, but as she looked up, she caught him flailing his arms back and forth.

"Are you OK?"

"Fine," Norman replied, digging his fork back into the meatloaf. "Maybe a little dry tonight?"

"Maybe," Ellie said. "The beef looked a bit old in the case."

The plan—never stated, but understood between them—had been for children, somewhere between several and a bunch. They weren't exactly trying from the get-go, but neither were they using protection. At first, they rationalized, Norman was moving up the ladder and when children did arrive they'd have increased security and stability; God would grant them their blessings when they were ready to receive them. After a while, it seemed strange, though, all that activity with nothing (not nothing, but you know . . .) to show for it. Norman first turned to God, praying, not for his sake, but Ellie's. When that didn't work, and they felt the window of opportunity closing, they went to the doctor, a humiliation.

They handed Norman a cup with a screw-top lid, his name, and a six-digit number written on the side, and showed him to a room with a reclining chair, a couch, and an array of skin magazines in a rack on the wall. It wasn't that Norman never masturbated, but he certainly didn't make a habit of it and did his best to think of Ellie when he did so. The magazines looked old, the pages worn. The women seemed eager to show the viewer their privates, making sure everything was spread for examination. They were shaved almost entirely, save a little column that looked to Norman like exclamation point. Norman realized he had never seen Ellie *down there.* He'd felt it, of course, and once or twice—more out of duty than desire—used his mouth, but it was always dark when they made love and when he tried it, Ellie would pull his head away and he would mount.

The pictures did nothing for Norman except make him shudder, but as he closed his eyes and tried to conjure Ellie, she stayed fuzzy and out of reach, so he reached for one of the magazines and turned to a page where the woman had one arm slung under her breasts, pushing them up and together, while her fingers reached for her privates. Norman folded the page so her lower half was covered and soon made his deposit, the spunk sad and gray under the overhead fluorescents. When he was done, not knowing why, he carefully tore the page from the magazine and folded it until it fit into a slot in his wallet.

The doctors said that individually there was nothing wrong with Norman and Ellie, but a fluke of body chemistry made his sperm incompatible with her womb. Ellie reached for Norman's hand and began to cry. Norman gripped it back and nodded stoically. The doctors said that when Norman's swimmers entered Ellie they became disoriented, like they were drunk, and swam the wrong direction or in circles. It was rare, the doctor said, but they did see this from time to time. Some remedies were being tried for this condition, but as of yet, nothing had proven promising. Still, conception was not impossible. Some of the sperm seemed to get the gist, just not enough to make the odds good. The doctor smiled at them and said, "The only thing to do is just keep trying, and have fun doing it!"

They were counseled on in vitro fertilization, but when they were told what happened to the leftover embryos, that was the end of that. You can't kill ten babies to make one and feel good about it.

For a while they did not try, Ellie turning her back to Norman as she slid under the sheets, a cool wall of air separating them. In the middle of the night Norman would wake with an erection and clenched fists. After several months, Ellie began throwing a leg over his body as they slept, and finally, one early morning just before dawn, he felt Ellie's hand groping at his legs and they were together again. They tried and tried, less often but regularly, and there were a few what they dubbed close calls but were just late periods, nothing close at all. One day they realized they'd both crossed forty-five and the odds had gone from negligible to nonexistent and that even adoption, at least of an infant, was a long shot. Norman did his best to count his blessings: health, a wife whom he loved and who loved him, success in business. To complain seemed ungracious, and yet he often thought about how unfair it seemed. Deep down he knew he had what it took to be a good father: the capacity for love, a willingness to sacrifice, a deep sense of ethics and morality, the instinct to protect combined with an openness to letting go when the time was right. Norman knew that fatherhood would be *fulfilling,* the end point of his destiny, and he was pretty sure Ellie felt the same about motherhood.

After it became apparent that their life together would be childless, without saying a word to each other they stopped trying. This is not to say that they never made love—they were human beings with needs—but each year Norman felt more and more of the need leaking out of him. But his love for Ellie did not diminish, even as his desire was slowly extinguished.

He shouldn't have had so much to drink. Normally he limited himself to one glass of wine, two at most if the dinner was going to be a prolonged one. They had been drinking cocktails that ended in "tini" and looked radioactive in the glass, and Norman had lost count at six. He knew he was talking too loud and too much, regaling the team—Bart, Laurie, Sheila, Ian, Scarlet, and of course Gina—with ancient tales from the company offices. He spilled secrets, some of which weren't his to give away, and after each story he saw them look at each other as if to say, "Get a load of this," before goading him on. He felt like a racehorse being spurred by the jockey. It was a large table, and he sat at the head with Gina on his right. At some point, hidden by the cloth, she'd put her hand on his knee, but he didn't miss a beat. When the waiter came to clear the dinner plates, Norman had hardly eaten any of his steak and *pommes frites,* but he sent the food away anyway and launched into another story. It felt like he'd been waiting his whole life to be in this place, with these people, *his* people, hanging on his experiences, his wisdom. Bart suggested a digestif, and when Norman stood to retire to the bar the room swirled and he clutched the table and he felt Gina reach for his elbow, keeping him steady.

Leaving the table broke the spell, though, and in the bar, the others picked up the conversation, airing typical workplace complaints about nonunderstanding bosses and stupid managerial moves. Norman, feeling wobbly, was rooted to a stool, afraid to stand. While he cringed a little at the criticism rained down on his longtime friends and colleagues, Norman felt flattered they would air these grievances in front of him, making it clear that he, Norman, was one of the good guys. He tried his best to nod or smile at the right spots without seeming too eager. One by one they excused themselves for the evening, until Norman was alone with Gina and she came to his stool and put her knee between his legs.

"I guess I'm just not tired yet. Are you?" she asked.

Norman shook his head. He was not tired; he was exhausted. He'd long ago lost track of the time, but he was certain he hadn't been up this late in years. It was a joke between him and Ellie that they celebrated New Year's on Greenwich Mean Time. Norman's hand clutched an empty glass that he didn't remember drinking from. He'd never been close to this drunk. The alcohol churned in his stomach.

"You know what turns me on?" Gina said.

Norman shook his head. He felt emptied.

"I love it when I know that someone really *wants* me. It's just the biggest turn-on. Don't get me wrong, you're not a bad-looking guy, Norm, but it doesn't matter because I see the way you look at me. It's like you don't want to admit how much you want me, but you can't contain it. It's just pouring out of you, and that drives me crazy."

Norman nodded.

"I had a shrink who called it a pathology. Can you believe that?" Gina said. "He said I mistook sex for love, but I don't even know what that means. You know?" Gina had pulled a small compact out of her purse. She examined herself in the mirror and frowned briefly before snapping it shut.

"I better go freshen up," she said. "You'll be OK here, won't you?"

As Gina turned for the bathroom, Norman's stomach flipped and he was sure he was going to vomit. It was imperative that he make it outside. He clamped his hand over his nose and mouth and ran, knocking into people, but even as he crested the door it came forth, spurting between his fingers out of his mouth and nose. The second and third and subsequent waves hit as he hunched over the curb. Strings of drool reached from his mouth toward the ground, and the stomach acid burned his nasal passages. He couldn't bear to have Gina see him this way, but neither could he move from the spot.

After a while he smelled her behind him, her fresh application of perfume penetrating even the smell of the upchuck. "I got sick," he said.

"Yeah, wow," Gina replied. "I can see that." After a long pause filled by only the sound of Norman spitting into the gutter, she said, "Is there something I can do?" in a way that made clear she didn't want to do anything.

"I'll see you in the office on Monday," Norman said, never turning around. He listened to her heels click away down the sidewalk, gaining speed with each step. He remained hunched until he felt strong hands tugging under his armpits, and he turned and saw the one in the lime-green sweater helping him upright.

"Upsie-daisy," the man said.

Norman cupped the coffee mug in his hands, not yet able to make himself drink.

"Go on," the lime-green-sweater said. "Drink up, you'll feel better."

They were in a diner, Norman across a booth from the one in the lime-green sweater and one of the ones that looked like just about anyone. Norman's tie was crusted with puke, ruined. He took it off and shoved it in his pocket. He'd drop it in the garbage on the way out.

"Ellie's got to be worried," Norman said.

"She's OK," lime-green-sweater replied.

"How do you know?"

"She trusts you."

Norman humphed at the irony and tried a sip of the coffee. It burned on the way down, and he added some cream from the little tin container on the table, swirling it through with his spoon. "So what do you want?" Norman said.

"What everyone else wants."

"And what's that?"

"Legal recognition of our bond. The state's seal on our love." The one with the lime-green sweater placed his hand gently on his partner's arm as he said this. They leaned together and touched heads. Norman thought it wasn't a bad-looking picture. He knew what that was.

"Love doesn't need official recognition," Norman grumbled.

"You're right," the one in the lime-green sweater replied. "Love is love is love. We don't *need* recognition, but we want it."

"Not everyone gets what they want."

"But why should we be denied our wants when they're the same as everybody else's?"

"Because it's not natural?"

"And who's to say what's natural?"

Norman tried to think, but his brain wasn't working quite right. It was late and he was confused and they were taking advantage of that and they kept touching each other in tender ways, which was distracting. "I'm sure there's an answer," he said, "but I can't think of it right now."

Both men smiled at Norman, the kind of look you give a child, and the one in the lime-green sweater spoke. "Well, you let us know when you do. We've been waiting a long time."

Norman nodded. He was tired of looking at them. They'd seen what happened with Gina, and that meant they reminded him of his shame. No one did any more talking. Some food Norman didn't remember ordering arrived, steak and eggs over easy, crispy hash browns that the yolk dripped through. Norman was suddenly hungry, so he ate, eyes on the plate, shoveling it in. The men must've left at some point because when he looked up, they were gone.

Making sure of sobriety, he slept in his car for an hour before driving home. He showered in the dark, slowly. He knew Ellie wasn't asleep when he slipped under the covers, but neither of them said anything.

The next morning, Norman slept late, and when he got up and went to the kitchen he saw Ellie scrubbing at the sink. "You hungry?" she called out without turning.

He went to her and pressed against his wife from behind and she stopped scrubbing, clutching the brush in her hand. Norman paused until he felt their breathing join, and he slipped one hand around front and through her robe and cupped her breast and Ellie dropped the scrub brush. Norman's other hand rested on Ellie's buttocks and then began to bunch the robe higher and with it the nightgown. He ran a finger along the inside of her thigh. Ellie sighed softly under his touch.

"What's got into you?" she said.

"Something," Norman replied.

My Best Seller

I'm going to write a best seller.

Because women buy most of the books, my best seller will have a female protagonist.

I'm going to call her Greta because I've always thought Greta is a pretty name.

In addition, I have become aware that the supernatural is hot, that people enjoy elements of mystery and magic in their best-selling books, that otherworldly creatures have a romantic appeal while also providing avenues for surprising turns of plot since supernatural creatures, by definition, are not bound by our natural world. However, the most common supernatural creatures—werewolves, vampires, witches, elves/orcs, and dragons—while "hot," are also said to be potentially "overdone," or "spent." Above all, my best seller will be original, so my best seller will not have any werewolves, vampires, witches, elves/orcs, or dragons.

Therefore, the protagonist of my best seller will be a female yeti, also known as a Sasquatch, by the name of Greta. The working title (tentative) will be *Bigfoot Woman.*

Greta may or may not have a pet unicorn.

It has come to my attention that a good strategy for a best-selling book is to write in a way that will appeal to young adults and adults alike, primarily (though not exclusively) women. This makes sense when one realizes that adults are just grown-up children, most (but not all) of whom would prefer to return to their childhoods because deep inside we all retain a child's sense of wonder. If there's any doubt about this, go to the Fourth of July fireworks and tell me there aren't plenty of grown-ups going "ooh" and "ahh" at the rockets' red glare and bombs bursting in the air.

So the protagonist of my best seller is now a *teenage* yeti named Greta who may or may not have a pet unicorn. For obvious reasons, the working title has changed from *Bigfoot Woman* to *Bigfoot Girl*.

All good books have conflict, and one form of conflict is internal conflict, something that goes on inside all of us, unseen but also unavoidable. Often, writers draw on their own experience when developing conflict. An example of an internal conflict is a writer trying to decide what kind of book to write. I have decided to write a best seller, so I have no more internal conflict, thus I will have to look elsewhere for Greta's conflict. Since Greta is a teenager, and teenagers often struggle over issues of identity, I've decided that this is what Greta will struggle with. In order to make this struggle more apparent and accessible to my reading audience of young and not young—primarily but not exclusively—female readers, my protagonist will be a teenage *half-yeti, half-human* female named Greta.

I'm starting to have strong doubts about the pet unicorn, unless it can also talk, or perhaps read minds, or maybe change colors depending on Greta's mood, which would be an interesting way of symbolizing Greta's conflict come to think about it.

What you've seen right there is what we writers call "creativity," real seat-of-the-pants invention-type stuff where you're just letting your mind go and seeing what connections it can make. I was about to ditch the pet unicorn, but instead I made it many times better. It's an incredible thing. This is one of the chief pleasures of writing, second only to getting official notification that the book you've written is a best seller. You should try it.

My half-human, half-yeti teenage protagonist Greta will be struggling over her identity: Namely, is she human, or is she yeti? Some reviewers will surmise that this internal conflict is analogous to someone's struggle over their sexuality or racial identity, and because I am savvy (a prerequisite for writing a best seller), I will let them say these things, even though they'll be wrong. Greta's internal struggle will be over whether she is human or yeti and nothing else.

Some things just are what they are.

My best seller will need a setting, a place for my character to engage in action. I am choosing the setting before I develop the action because good writers know that action does not come first. Action flows out of character, conflict, and place. The story of a half-yeti, half-human teenage female named Greta in outer space would entail very different actions than the story of a half-yeti, half-human teenage female named Greta in Mumbai, India.

I have decided that the setting for my best seller will be high school.

Instinctively I know that this is a good choice, for several reasons. One, my audience of young and not young—primarily but not exclusively—female readers will either currently be in or have been to high school and will instantly relate to the various goings-on in my best seller about the story of a half-yeti, half-human teenage female named Greta.

Two, I have been to high school and am therefore familiar with the setting, limiting the need for research, which would be intensive and time-consuming if my setting was something like outer space or Mumbai, India, places I've never been, nor particularly want to go.

Third, this adds an exciting new element to my best seller's continually evolving working title, *Bigfoot Girl Goes to High School*.

And finally, even as I decided that the setting would be high school, I began to see potential for happenings that will transform Greta's internal conflict into external dramatic action. For example, because of her half-yeti heritage Greta will be quite tall and unusually strong, but she will also hate basketball and will therefore have to deal with the constant pleas to join the team from the coach, Ms. Franchione, who is convinced that with Greta patrolling the middle, her team would have a real shot at the state championship.

Ms. Franchione will also recognize that being a basketball star would help Greta with her issues of identity, since Greta would then see herself in terms of her abilities, rather than her mixed genetic heritage—like how I self-identify as "writer of a best seller," so anything else you may find out about me becomes irrelevant.

I am also envisioning a scene where Greta is publicly and humiliatingly ostracized, not only because it would be a manifestation and intensification of her internal conflict regarding her half-yeti, half-human status, but also because at some point during high school, *all* girls are publicly and humiliatingly ostracized, usually, and ironically, by their friends.

All best-selling books employ irony.

I'm thinking there will be a moment when Greta and Laura, Greta's best childhood friend and neighbor, will be entering a bathroom, and loud enough for everyone to hear, Laura will turn to Greta and say, "The sign on the door says 'girls' not 'freaks.'" In the moment, Greta will be shocked and silent, since the comment has cut to the core of her own doubts about herself. On the way home, as the pent-up tears flow down her cheeks, she will overturn several cars, which will cause her mother significant trouble because she will have to make restitution to the owners.

Notice how my choices of character—a half-yeti, half-human female named Greta—and setting—high school—for my best seller have given birth to several supporting characters: Ms. Franchione, Laura, and now Greta's mother. Of these, Greta's mother will be the most important, and therefore she will have significant conflicts of her own. Greta's mother will be an ex–beauty pageant contestant who retains traces of her loveliness, but has been mostly worn down by the struggle of being a single mother to a half-yeti, half-human female named Greta. Greta's mother will be named Tammy, because this is an appropriate name for an aging beauty who works waiting tables in a restaurant that is probably a diner.

I haven't forgotten about the unicorn. It's going to be half the size of a Chihuahua, and Greta will keep it in her backpack. This makes sense and will be compelling to my audience of young and not young—primarily but not exclusively—female readers because I will claim that unicorns are not imaginary at all, but rather quite common, and the problem is that we don't spend enough time looking at the ground to see them. I'm envisioning a product tie-in, which is not my area of expertise, but seems pretty obvious.

You know, plush toys.

I haven't forgotten about plot, either. Many books are published without plots, but very few best-selling books are absent plot. Plot is not to be confused with action or story. Action is stuff that happens. Story is the sum total of the action. Plot is action that happens because one action *caused* another action. The classic example to illustrate this distinction is that story is, "The queen died, then the king died." Plot is, "The queen died and then the king died *of grief* (resulting in his kingdom falling into disarray until his brother, Yardrick the Somewhat Fair, makes a play for the throne which starts a war and other stuff)."

To apply this to the writing of my best seller, story is, "I wrote a bestseller." Plot is, "Because of the writing of a bestseller, I got rich and had to hire an accountant to keep track of all of my money."

An underappreciated aspect of writing a best seller is the choice of font. I choose Garamond, a very old typeface that conveys a sense of fluidity and consistency.

It looks like this.

Romance. I'm going to need a romance, since, after all, my best seller is intended for an audience of young and not young—primarily but not exclusively—female readers who like romance and have a thirst for love. (Male readers also have a thirst for love, but they're less likely to admit it. Very few males will purchase my best seller—or when they do, they will claim it is as a gift—but many more will read it, sneaking it off the shelves after the women in their lives have finished.)

Romance comes in two forms, requited and unrequited, and my best seller will have one of each since they both provide compelling emotional reading experiences, experiences that are further heightened when placed in juxtaposition.

The (ultimately) requited romance will involve my protagonist, the half-human, half-yeti female named Greta, and the high school's star athlete, Jimmy. In order to keep Jimmy from being a cliché he will be not a quarterback, but a running back, and also be up for the yearly science prize and an academic scholarship for his project on sequencing DNA. It is Jimmy's prowess with genotyping that initially attracts Greta to Jimmy since he may provide a key to unlocking her true identity, but mostly she likes how his eyes are kind, and she just wants to go to prom, where she, rather than Laura, will be crowned queen and have a dance with the smartest and handsomest boy in the school (Jimmy). My audience of young and not young—primarily but not exclusively—female readers will like this because it is a conclusion that implies a kind of cosmic order, a reassurance that love can conquer all in a frequently chaotic world.

The working title for my best seller is now *Bigfoot Girl Wants to Go to Prom.*

The unrequited romance will involve Greta's mother, Tammy, and Greta's father, whose name is unpronounceable as it consists of a series of guttural noises generally not producible by the human anatomy, so we'll call him Phil. When Tammy was in high school herself, she became lost in the woods during a family camping trip. She had left camp to gather firewood, but soon found herself trapped, her foot hopelessly pinned under a log. As night fell, exhausted from her struggles to free herself and crying out for help, she lost consciousness, wondering if she'd ever awake. As she slept, Phil came upon her and lifted the log off her foot and gently carried her back to his lair, where he laid her in a bed of leaves near the fire and placed a poultice on her swollen ankle and administered drops of water to her parched lips from a hollowed-out log.

When Tammy awakes, she sees Phil and is not afraid, which is pretty much a first for Phil when it comes to encounters with humans. Tammy spends seven days with Phil in his lair, during which time they make sweet, interspecies love often, as though their coupling has been cast by the Fates themselves. Ultimately, though, the search party looking for Tammy comes increasingly close to Phil's lair and there is an increasingly serious danger that Phil will be found out, that he will be captured and imprisoned and become a permanent object of scientific study. Though Tammy and Phil cannot actually talk to each other because they do not share a verbal language, their touch and the looks in their eyes make it clear that there is only one, tragic choice to be made, that Tammy must leave the lair, allow herself to be found, lie about the circumstances of her survival, and ultimately, eleven months later when Greta is born (yeti gestation time is longer than human) say that the father is "just some dumb boy" she wants nothing to do with. Because Tammy has been through a terrible trauma, people will choose to believe her, even though when she is born, Greta weighs nearly sixteen pounds and is covered head to toe in a light fur.

Whoa. That even began to get to me a little. This is exciting. I can't wait to start writing my best seller. I think maybe I will tell the publisher to print my best seller on paper that is especially absorbent in order to sop up the likely tears of my young and not young—primarily but not exclusively—female readers.

One of the important things to do when writing a best seller is to decide which common elements of best sellers to *leave out* of my best seller. Therefore, my best seller will not have the following: sword fights, time travel, secret societies, clones, profanity.

Though even as I type this, I am reconsidering the exclusion of secret societies, since a secret society of yeti-hunters, perhaps led by the father of Laura, former best friend and then rival of Greta, my half-yeti, half-human female protagonist, could provide an interesting and dangerous subplot.

What this goes to show is that there's no real formula to writing a best seller. The moment you think you're not going to do something, bam! You wind up doing it.

My best seller is going to need a climax, and looking at my plans for my best seller I can already see the seeds of something that will be really whiz-bang.

It will happen on prom night. Many things have come to a head all together. Tammy, Greta's mother, will at last confirm what Greta has long suspected about her parentage, that she is the product of the coupling of human and yeti. On the one hand, she will be relieved to finally know the truth. On the other hand, it turns out that she really is kind of a freak. At the same time, the pressure on Greta's mother, Tammy, to repay the owners of the overturned cars damaged by Greta following her confrontation with her former best friend, Laura, is growing more serious, with the sheriff threatening to arrest Tammy if she can't come up with restitution.

In the meantime Laura's father, head of the secret society of yeti hunters, is aware that Jimmy is sequencing Greta's DNA, and he plans on stealing the final genetic analysis in order to prove Greta's true nature. Laura's father, wielding the data printout from Jimmy's machine, plans to interrupt prom night by capturing Greta and taking her back to the secret society for further study. In his head he has rehearsed his triumphant line, "This is no prom queen! This is a monster!"

Guilt-ridden by the fact that her mother is going to pay the consequences for Greta's destruction of the automobiles and simultaneously curious about and embittered at her father, on prom night Greta hatches a plan to find him in the woods, confront him about his absence from her life, and also take his picture which she will sell to a tabloid for enough money to pay for the damaged autos. She is hoping all of this can be wrapped up in time for her to make the announcement of prom queen and have a dance with Jimmy, her true love.

Relying on her half-yeti instincts, Greta is able to find her father's lair and upon confronting him discovers that she can actually speak passable yeti. She finds out her father, who we're calling Phil, never knew of her existence and is overjoyed to discover that he has a daughter. After a long and loving embrace, Greta explains Tammy's situation to Phil (in yeti), and he agrees to let his picture be taken in order to raise the money, so long as it is from a sufficient distance and kind of blurry.

At this moment, Greta's tiny unicorn will have a golden, kind of buttery glow, which will symbolize love and also togetherness.

But just as Greta is to bid farewell to her father and return to town in order to dress for the prom where she will be crowned queen and dance with her true love Jimmy, they will hear the advance of a strike team from the secret yeti-hunting society. The strike team has been able to follow Greta's trail because, as only half-yeti, she is not as skilled at covering her tracks as her father, and in a parallel to the earlier flashback scene where Phil and Greta's mother, Tammy, are almost found out, a sudden sacrifice must be made. This time it is Phil who makes it, charging out of his lair while unleashing his fiercest yeti bellow and attempting to lead the secret society strike team deeper and deeper into the woods, away from his daughter so her secret will not be discovered. In the lair, Greta will hear the gunshots of the strike team echoing farther and farther in the distance as her father runs for his life.

While this is happening, Jimmy discovers Laura's father's plan to reveal Greta's mixed-species DNA at prom, so Jimmy alters his DNA sequencer to produce a false result declaring that Greta is actually a marsupial. This will sabotage Laura's father's plan and make him look foolish in front of everyone at the prom, but it also torpedoes Jimmy's hopes for an academic scholarship, which would have allowed him to quit playing football, which he secretly loathes.

Like I said, irony.

Sadly, all this prom night activity causes both Greta and Jimmy to miss the dance, so when they are announced as queen and king a single spotlight will shine on the empty gym floor. The best seller will end with Tammy making her way home from the woods and Jimmy sitting alone in his lab.

It's hard to express how much fun it has been to write about writing my best seller. In fact, it has been so much fun that I'm not much looking forward to actually writing my best seller anymore. One of the cruel ironies about writing is that the idea, the conception, the vision, never quite gets on the page in quite the way it exists in the writer's mind, and in writing about writing my best seller, I realize that this is inevitably the case here. Greta and Tammy and Phil and Jimmy and Laura and Laura's father and Ms. Franchione and the yeti-hunting secret-society strike team are very much alive inside me—I feel their presences very, very deeply. Some writers talk about bringing their characters to life on the page, but I'm afraid that at this point the writing would, in reality, be the slow process of killing them, and I'm not sure I'm prepared to do that.

I've got a lot of respect for the people who do write best sellers. They must have a ruthlessness that I lack.

But fortunately, look at all the questions I've left myself. Did Phil escape the strike team to possibly reunite with Greta and Tammy? Will Laura's father discover Greta's secret? If you are not there to receive the prom queen's crown, are you still the prom queen? And most of all, I recognize that my previously planned requited love has been left unrequited. When all is said and done, will Jimmy and Greta find true love with each other?

All these questions have a significant upside, namely the need for a sequel, which I am going to start writing about right now. It is going to be called *Bigfoot Girl Goes to College*.

Notes from a Neighborhood War

Billy Turner and Jimmy Elliott were ten years old.

"Oh yeah?" Billy Turner said to Jimmy Elliott.

"Yeah!" Jimmy Elliott said back to Billy Turner as he kicked Billy in the shin and then socked him in the gut, dropping him to the sidewalk. Billy held his shin with one hand and his stomach with the other and moaned up from the ground.

"I'm going to get my brother and have him beat you up."

Which he did.

Billy went home and got his older brother, Sam, who was fourteen and had hair under his arms. Sam and Billy walked over to the Elliott home and rang the doorbell. When Jimmy answered the door, Sam dragged him outside, pushed him to the ground, and held Jimmy down with his left hand while blackening the boy's eye and bloodying his nose with his right.

Jimmy looked up at the Turners and vowed, "My brother can beat up your brother."

Which was true, if half-brothers count, because Jimmy's half-brother Andrew was thirty-two years old, an investment banker living in a different city a plane ride away who had played some college football (Division II, but still . . .) and continued to work out four days a week. Jimmy called Andrew on the phone, after which Andrew hopped on a direct flight, stopping at home just long enough to collect Jimmy and head over to the Turners'.

Billy answered the door and declared that Sam was not home, but Sam was indeed home, hiding under the bed, the third place Andrew

Elliott looked. Andrew dragged Sam Turner out from under the bed and proceeded to kick a few of the boy's teeth down his throat. Billy Turner looked down at his brother on the floor, then back up at Jimmy and Andrew Elliott and shouted, "Well, my dad can beat up your brother!"

This was a more dubious proposition.

Billy and Sam's father, Earl Turner, was in charge of accounts receivable at the local tool-and-dye, and at night as he changed for bed and looked at himself in the golden glow of the bathroom vanity, he saw breasts. Fortunately, one of the tools they manufactured at the local tool-and-dye was tire irons. Making sure to put the tire iron in his checked baggage, Earl Turner flew to Atlanta, signed in at the security desk of Columbus, Cornell, and Hum Financial Services, LLC, sneaked up behind Andrew Elliott, older half-brother of Jimmy Elliott, and cracked his skull with the tire iron, leaving him slumped and bleeding over his computer keyboard.

Upon hearing this news, Jimmy Elliott was at a loss, for he had no father. Jimmy was the product of a second marriage by his (and Andrew's) now-deceased father to Jimmy's much younger mother. Luckily, Jimmy had recently completed a school unit on civics, and during those lessons he learned that our government works for the people, even individual people younger than voting age, and that when individual people have problems, they can and should contact their congressional representative.

Congressperson Maxine Williams was Jimmy's second call. His first was to Billy Turner.

"My duly elected representative can beat up your father!" he shouted into the phone before hanging up on Billy Turner.

Congressperson Williams enjoyed a good fight, though she was not one for actual fisticuffs, for she favored elaborate hats that were easily dented. However, she was on the Subcommittee for Domestic Military Preparedness, which meant she had the e-mail address for a couple of National Guard colonels. Col. Evan Smith, Army Reserves, also enjoyed a good fight, as well as armor-plated vehicles, which his unit happened to be short on, a problem that was soon remedied thanks to the influence of Congressperson Williams after Strike Team Omega rappelled through a hole blown in the roof of Cornell Brothers Tool & Dye into the glassed-in office of Earl Turner and "eliminated" their target with minimal collateral damage.

Billy Turner would not stand for this. Billy called the number in the advertisement from the back of *Soldiers for Hire* magazine, the one that said, at the bottom, "Blood is thicker than water, but money is thicker than blood." Billy met Mr. Hawk at midnight behind the Gas & Guzzle and showed Mr. Hawk the life-insurance check issued after his father's "elimination," while in exchange Mr. Hawk showed Billy the skull tattoos on his knuckles and how his knife blade glinted green and deadly under the phosphorus lamps of the Gas & Guzzle lot.

Back home, Billy smiled as he dialed the familiar numbers of Jimmy Elliott. "My hired mercenaries can take out your National Guard strike team!"

Click.

And boy, did they, at least as far as anyone could tell. One by one, as the strike team members slept, or carried groceries in from the car, or pushed their daughter on a swing in the local park, they were "disappeared," just as Mr. Hawk promised.

Neither Jimmy Turner nor the National Guard nor Rep. Williams was going to take this lying down, but neither were they going to find Mr. Hawk and his team of professional ghosts, so instead they took their new armor-plated vehicles and drove them straight through the Elliotts' front window, and the front windows of two of the Elliotts' neighbors for good measure. Jimmy was at school, and thus escaped harm, but the collateral damage was considerable this time.

At that point things started to get serious; sides were chosen, lines drawn, loyalties demanded and declared. The war spread past the neighborhood to the surrounding community, the bordering counties, the tri-state area, the region, the country, the continent, the world . . .

An orphan now, Jimmy Elliott was adopted by the CEO of a major supplier to the military/industrial complex who recognized a good opportunity when he saw one. Jimmy now had a warm bed, three square meals a day, and a direct pipeline to an undersecretary for policy and procurement.

Strike followed counterstrike, and as the years passed, the war's origins were forgotten, but what was clear was that the other side was hateful, godless, and evil, that they loathed those things we cherished and wished to subjugate us to their will, push us into the sea, end our way of life as we knew it, and our calling to resist and defeat every last one of them was a divine one, irrefutable and true.

At various times, international oversight bodies chided, admonished, reprimanded, reproved, and rebuked both sides. The leaders of the great powers condemned the senseless killings in the harshest possible language.

"We condemn these senseless killings in the harshest possible language," they said.

As much ink as blood was spilled discussing the "problem," but words crumbled in the face of this neighborhood war. Occasionally there were talks, discussions, summits, frameworks, road maps, once even a handshake, but each time the peace was bruised, or broken, or—one time—shattered.

The problem is they won't give in, Billy Turner announced.

The problem is they won't quit, Jimmy Elliott told anyone who asked.

Generations born into the war were called upon to fight and paid the ultimate sacrifice. "We honor those who have paid the ultimate sacrifice," everyone said. This, at least, was widely agreed upon.

But nights, Jimmy Elliott and Billy Turner paced the floors of their command center secure rooms in their respective strongholds, surrounded by advisors who frowned down as they shuffled and reshuffled their stacks of intelligence. "Does this look right side up to you?" the advisors asked each other, turning the pages this way and that.

Troubled, deeply troubled, Jimmy Elliott and Billy Turner turned away from their advisors and stroked the grayed stubble on their chins and caught a glance of their sagging faces in their lighted real-time situation maps.

Look at how my ears droop, like an elephant's, Jimmy Elliot marveled.

When did my neck wattle like that? Billy Turner wondered.

I am an old, old man, they both thought.

They stood up straight, locking their spines and clicking their feet together and they pushed the heels of their hands into their eyes and rubbed as though trying to wake from a dream and looked again at the real-time situation maps, and they both said out loud, though not loud enough for anyone to hear, "We're losing."

Tuesday, the Bad Zoo

Feeling the approaching jet as only an ominous rumbling that shakes her subterranean, brick-walled lab, Dr. Thornwood, Jane, lifts a blackened organ from the most recently deceased lynx and weighs it on the overhead scale. Jane sighs and pushes her glasses up on her nose with the back of her wrist as she records the organ's weight and prepares it for sectioning and closer examination.

Elsewhere, Zoo Director Watkins holds the phone receiver out to the Visiting Dignitary as though he wishes to be bludgeoned with it. To the Visiting Dignitary, the tired voice on the phone says: *Your suit is buttoned improperly. Do it right. It's not dignified. Now give me back to the Zoo Director.*

To the Zoo Director, the tired voice says: *What you're thinking of doing tonight, don't. You'd regret it. There's always consequences. In other news, the ibex is about to . . .*

. . . but the remainder of the tired voice's words are squelched by the 8:23 on approach to runway LX-49er. Zoo Director Watkins watches his office windows bow and flex from the jet blast, and he wonders when the windows will finally give up and bust into shards and kill him already.

Meanwhile, the Visiting Dignitary dives for the floor.

Oblivious as the plane passes, Walter works the nozzle on his helium tank and reads that day's first memo from marketing:

Henceforth, until notified further, Tuesdays will be "one balloon for one penny" day, meaning that the first balloon purchased by any given individual will be for the sum of one penny. Upon completion of each balloon transaction, the balloon purchaser should be advised that "All sales are final and carry no warranties or guarantees."

By way of example, this means that should a "dolphin" or "panda" or "lemur" balloon (remember to feature the "lemur," as we are in a current state of glut on this item) be purchased by a mewling, soot-covered moppet who has successfully wheedled a penny from its mother or father or temporary caregiver, they having given in to the child's pleadings quite easily, actually, with a penny being less than inconsequential and all, should said balloon, we don't know . . . explode, the second (as well as any subsequent) balloon will cost $45.

There are no exceptions, ever.

After he finishes reading the memo, Walter initials the bottom, indicating that he has understood and does not need or want further clarification, and will comply with its wishes.

Jane loves Walter in a deep and abiding way. Walter is also deeply in love with Jane, but neither of them knows this about the other, thinking (for different reasons) that the other could never possibly be interested in them, which is a shame, but not uncommon in today's world.

Digging fingers into the thin office shag, the Visiting Dignitary yelps, and tries to climb farther under his chair as the flaps on the 8:23 thud into landing position. The Zoo Director shouts something, perhaps helpful, at the Visiting Dignitary, but cannot be heard above the din. From the office floor, the Visiting Dignitary looks up at Zoo Director Watkins with the moist and pleading eyes of someone who is certain that a jet airplane is about to land on top of him.

Walter reads the second memo from Marketing:

We have given the aforementioned "lemur" glut some further thought and we are very pleased with ourselves. Very pleased indeed.

Henceforth, the "lemur" balloon will now be renamed and sold not as a "lemur," but as a mutant "monkey-fox" created through genetic mutation triggered by high doses of radiation. Upon inflation, all "monkey-fox" balloons should now be decorated with the attached "lightning bolt" stickers.

Sighing, Walter initials the bottom.

The impossible shriek of moving parts working hard, working fast to keep a heavy object aloft, reaches its peak as the 8:23 passes over the Zoo Director's office. Zoo Director Watkins comes around the desk, kneels beside the Visiting Dignitary, puts an arm around his shoulders, and shouts into his ear: *Do not be alarmed! From this close, they all sound like they're going to crash! But they never do! At least not yet! Maybe someday, though!*

The Visiting Dignitary nods. He touches his ear where the Zoo Director's warm breath has landed. He tries his hardest to believe.

Walter reads the day's last memo from marketing:

On Tuesdays, until notified further, all balloons will be inflated to 15PSI, which, it should be noted, is 3PSI higher than the normally recommended 12PSI.

There are no exceptions, ever.

As Walter initials the bottom, he thinks about Dr. Thornwood, Jane, and of course the talented penguin and that evening's plan that he and Jane have made together.

The plane passes over in a final, thundering whoosh, and in the relative silence of its wake, the Zoo Director's phone rings. Zoo Director Watkins nods and listens for a moment before holding the receiver out to the Visiting Dignitary as though he wishes to be strangled with the cord.

To the Visiting Dignitary the perturbed voice says: *Get off the floor. Now! You know why. Get a hold of yourself. Do you have your scissors?*

Rolling on the floor, the Visiting Dignitary pats his suit pockets, searching frantically for his scissors.

This is how the day begins at the bad zoo.

In nature, the ibex (a kind of wild goat with transversely ridged, re-curved horns that populates the high mountains of Asia Minor) is not known to cough. In fact, as they live in the wild as members of the ibex pack—scrambling across cragged peaks to forage for meals of moss or lichen—the ibex has never been observed coughing, but as the bad zoo's ibex stands perched at the apex of its artificially con-structed mountain, it watches the 11:34 circle into alignment for ap-proach and landing and begins to chuffle, just a little, under its breath.

Walter gingerly hands the 15PSI cheetah to a fat-faced boy, who in turn gives Walter a sticky penny. The boy's mother sits nearby, slumped on a bench, tilted slightly sideways. The cheetah, bulging and bloated, stares over the boy's shoulder at Walter as the boy weaves back to his weary mother, both hands clutched around the balloon's string.
    All sales are final! Walter calls after the boy, cupping his hand to his mouth to be better heard over the plane. *No warranties or guarantees!*
    Hearing the words just vaguely, the boy turns back to Walter, and in so doing, trips . . .

In her lab, Jane, nearly disappeared inside a storage closet, digs un-derneath bags of wet and moldy wood shavings until she finds the bolt cutters.

As the 11:34 pulls closer, the ibex coughs even harder, then ducks its head to its shoulder, coughing still, and begins to tremble.

The boy falls, and the balloon pops. The boy cries from the startle of the balloon bursting as he rubs his slightly hurt knee.

In the office, the Visiting Dignitary squeezes his finally found scissors and cowers now from the passing 11:34. Zoo Director Watkins closes his eyes, tilts back in his chair, and remembers the warm crackle on the line during his transatlantic call and the gruff and foreign voice on the other end giving affirmative answers to questions spoken in careful code. Pictures of swarthy men packing Stinger missiles in straw-filled crates, fashioned from unfinished wood, run through his head.

Landing gear grinding into locked position, the 11:34 passes overhead. An easy shot, he thinks. The Zoo Director smiles at the Visiting Dignitary, who asks: *Is it not time?*

Zoo Director Watkins nods. Soon, soon, he thinks.

The ibex's tremble progresses to a shake, and soon, spasms.

Dr. Thornwood, Jane, folds a fresh blanket and places it next to the bolt cutters as she haphazardly dictates her postmortem report for the most recently deceased lynx:

Sectioning and sample analysis of the major organs and tissues indicate that the subject suffered from near saturation of the petrochemical alkaloids, chlorides, and petroalkachlorides, causing total system shutdown. It is difficult to determine the origin for the subsequent organ failure, but circulation analysis indicates that most likely, the heart was the last to go.

You see, ma'am . . . Walter says to the fat-faced child's mother as she fans a small wad of limp bills before him. *I'd have to charge you $45 for the second balloon, that's just as clear as day in the memo—no guarantees and no warranties—but what I'm going to do here in a moment is take a lunch break where I'll sit elsewhere, well away from the tank and the balloons, which due to my inexplicable oversight, will stay here, unguarded. Do you see what I'm saying?*

The woman shrugs and shakes her head and points to the sky. The plane, it is too loud.

The 11:34 honks out a final belch of exhaust as it passes over Ibex Mountain. The ibex turns its head skyward and flares its nostrils at the tangy scent of wasted jet fuel and coughs even harder, from deeper in the lungs.

Trying a different approach, Walter gestures at the woman. He points at his watch, then holds his fingers very slightly apart before jerking a thumb over his shoulder, which he follows with exaggerated chewing motions. Walter then slaps the helium tank and shakes the balloon and points points points at the ground with both hands.

Yes! the woman shouts. She holds the sniveling child's hand and jumps in place.

Yes! Yes! Yes!

It's time now, Zoo Director Watkins says to the Visiting Dignitary, who rises, clicks his scissors, open then shut, and checks his suit buttons for the hundredth time.

The ibex takes one final, wracked breath, and in a clatter of horns and hooves tumbles down the artificial escarpment.

Zoo Director Watkins prepares to deliver his speech, wingmanned by the Visiting Dignitary, who holds his scissors poised over the red ribbon, waiting for the signal. The Visiting Dignitary concentrates on keeping his hand steady and his attention firmly on the Zoo Director's words so he may fulfill his obligation when he is called upon to do so.

Responding to some unknown cue, the group of thirty or so penguins leap from their white-painted concrete ledge into the water and swirl around the plexiglas tank for a few minutes before zipping from the water, back to the ledge, shaking feathers dry, and massing for a good stare at the arctic scene painted on the rear wall.

One of the penguins, the talented one, remains behind in the water, and is watched by Walter and Jane as they discuss that evening's plan.

You have everything? Walter asks.

Yes.

Are the cutters sharp? Is the blanket big enough?

Yes, Jane says. *Yes.*

Walter blushes as Jane softly brushes his hand.

The woman first fills a dozen or so cheetah balloons and ties them around the child's wrist, then turns to the panda balloons, another dozen or so, and ties this bunch to the child's other wrist, after which she stands, hands on hips, and surveys her boy.

Zoo Director Watkins has mostly forgotten what he was supposed to say, but says something anyway: *Here, in our zoo, today, ummm . . . this afternoon, we are so very, so pleased to announce the opening and dedication of our new habitat, uhhh, our new habitat in which we will have prairie dogs, I mean . . . our new prairie dog habitat.*

Zoo Director Watkins looks out and tries a weak smile before mustering the resolve to continue. *We have taken pains . . .*

The mother thumbs a smudge from the child's cheek. The animal balloons tied to his wrists bobble in the breeze as the woman bends and hefts her child. Light as a feather, she thinks.

The talented penguin arcs through the water, performing twisting loops, spirals, and rolls that make Walter and Jane look at each other and laugh.

Walter sits forward on the bench and presses his hand to the glass. *He's good, isn't he?*

Very.

What will we do afterwards?

We haven't thought that far, have we?

Should we?
No.
It won't stop us.
Right.
Right.

Walter turns to Jane and puts his hand on her knee. *I just did something, for someone,* he says. She moves closer and listens.

The woman ties the last of the animal balloons to the child's belt loops before taking out a lipstick and drawing two magenta arcs under each of his eyes and a downward-pointing triangle on the boy's brow. She angles the lightning bolt stickers down his cheeks and teases the child's hair until it stands straight, as though he's been shocked. Gripping the boy by the shoulders, the mother says what she said not so long ago as she watched in wonder while the child hauled himself up on the corner of the old, chipped end table (you know the one) and charged toward her with his great stamping feet and windmilling wild arms, his mouth open at the sheer surprise, at the audacity and daring of this act . . . this walking, and the mother clapped and shouted until finally, swallowing her child in her arms she said: *Look at my beautiful boy! My beautiful, beautiful world-beater boy!*

He's wonderful, Jane says.
   Do you think he does it for us?
   Yes. That is why we do things for others, to be noticed.
   I am noticing you, Walter says.

Sweating heavily, tortured by the crowd that looks at him strangely, Zoo Director Watkins wipes his brow with his sleeve and has still another go: *What I'm telling you is that in a couple minutes, when that truck over there backs up and drops its tailgate and unleashes those prairie dogs, those doggies are going to find not only the finest replicated midwestern prairie soil that science can give us and money can buy, but some really amazing tunnels, half a mile of tunnels, twisty ones, just like the prairie dogs like. We've taken real pains here, I mean, I've seen maps . . .*

There is a disturbance, and the crowd turns away from the Zoo Director.

The Visiting Dignitary shades his eyes with his hand and squints at the small figure that floats toward them.

The mother watches her child drift and claps and shouts over and over: *My boy! my boy! my boy!*

People point and murmur as the boy passes just overhead. Some jump and try to grab his feet. They fail. The Visiting Dignitary grips his scissors like a dagger and gauges the figure's approach, evaluates the potential threat. Zoo Director Watkins looks from the boy to the Visiting Dignitary clutching the scissors and simultaneously ducks (successfully) and tries (in vain) to grab the Visiting Dignitary's arm.

All the while the talented penguin swims and swims, and finally zooms toward the glass and touches where Walter and Jane press their hands. The talented penguin then jumps from the water, dances a quick jig from foot to foot, and extends a wing toward Walter and Jane, bowing its head just a bit.

Walter and Jane applaud until their hands hurt while behind them, the Zoo Custodian whistles to himself in low tones as he wheels the ibex by on a handcart, one hoof poking out from beneath a canvas shroud.

This is how the day ends at the bad zoo.

In his small apartment, the Visiting Dignitary stares at the gravy from his TV turkey dinner as it sloshes over into the applesauce compartment. The phone is unplugged; his suit sits balled in the corner.

Zoo Director Watkins rolls his head around his shoulders, shaking off this particular awful day, from a string of awful days; then, locked and loaded, but with safety on, he begins to climb Ibex Mountain.

Wielding the bolt cutters, Walter chews through the chain-link fence at the penguin compound. Jane carries the blanket stuffed beneath her jacket. Nearby, the custodian wheels his trash bin down the path, pausing to turn up the soft strains of mariachi music coming from his transistor radio. Jane leans over to check Walter's progress, causing her hair to fall across her shoulders and into Walter's face.

Unable to stem the gravy tide with his fork, the Visiting Dignitary eats the applesauce out of order and quickly, before it is ruined completely.

Oh, sorry, Jane says, fingering the hair back behind an ear. *I'm cursed with this fine hair, just like my mother and her mother before that. If they live long enough, the women in our family wind up practically bald. I remember this one aunt who couldn't go out in the summer without a hat on for fear of burning…*
    It's OK, Walter says. *I'm nervous too.*

Arm splinted to his chest, soothed by the narcotics, the boy sleeps in his hospital room, mouth open and snoring. In a chair beside the bed, the boy's mother sleeps as well. Her hand rests across the child's middle. The television shows a program where a man takes pies in the face over and over again.

I was fired, Walter says as he holds the clipped fencing back for Jane.
    Don't worry, I make a good wage, Jane says softly in return, slipping carefully through the opening.

The Visiting Dignitary brings the TV dinner tray to his face and licks each compartment—turkey with gravy, lima beans mixed with corn, applesauce, and finally peach brown betty—clean, and mutters to himself over and over: *These are the fruits of our labor, these are the fruits of our labor. I shall not want. These are the fruits of our labor.*

Out of breath, the Zoo Director straddles the peak of Ibex Mountain and swings the shoulder-mounted launcher into place. The night sky has been wiped free of stars by the bright city lights, and as he flips the scope down, he has little difficulty sighting the red and green blinkers of the 10:21. Late as usual, he thinks. The plane nearly fills the crosshairs as the Zoo Director tries to control his breathing.

As a boy, the Zoo Director had a slingshot, a good one given him by a young uncle who admonished his nephew not to tell his mother as he slipped it into the back pocket of the boy's jeans. For weeks, the Zoo Director sneaked from the house to plunk bottles and cans from stumps and ledges with whizzing shots of carefully chosen pebbles. His aim was very good. Deadeye, he called himself.

The talented penguin is waiting for them as Walter cuts the cage lock and Jane swings the door open. Jane bends down and holds the blanket wide, and the talented penguin hops into her arms.

Walter smiles broadly as he wipes the bolt cutters clean of prints and drops them to the floor. *OK then,* he says.

With a broom for his partner, the custodian clicks his heels in time to the mariachi music and dances as he sweeps into a small mound rubber shards that once were animal balloons.

Heads swiveling, senses alert, Walter and Jane hustle from the grounds. The penguin is swaddled in the blanket, clutched to Jane's chest.

Jane says, *He's so warm—feel.*

She stops, and Walter touches the bundle.

Whoa! he says, pulling his hand back and then touching again.

Yes. We must go. But where must we go? Walter asks. Jane hands the bundled penguin to Walter.

Follow.

When the Zoo Director was a boy, a large crow lived atop a bowed phone wire in the alley behind his home. The crow terrified the young Zoo Director, shrieking and beating its wings every time he would pass the garbage cans that served as the crow's well-stocked cupboard. Daily, as the Zoo Director tried a shortcut through the alley on the way to school, or the ball field, or to chase the chime of the ice cream wagon, the crow would swoop down, forcing the Zoo Director to turn back and take the long way around, causing him to be late, to miss important things.

Walter, Jane, and the penguin sit in the diner, cupping warm mugs of cocoa in their hands or flippers. The penguin looks from Walter to Jane and back again with his dark, unblinking eyes.

Where shall we start? Walter wonders.

Jane looks at the penguin and says: *Always stick to the crosswalks and look both ways first, and when the light's yellow, you must hurry to the other side. Green means go; red means stop. After preparing uncooked chicken, wipe down surfaces thoroughly, and do not reuse utensils without first washing. For meat, use a good thermometer to check for doneness. In a close game, with a runner on third and less than two outs, you must bring the infield in.*

The penguin keeps its eyes on Jane as it dips its beak to the cocoa.

The crow took tiny, mincing steps across the phone wire and weaved its head as the Zoo Director, one eye shut, took his aim. He had selected a largish stone with one rounded and one jagged edge. It looked lethal to him. He fitted the stone in the slingshot's pouch, pulled his arm back, and released in a single motion, and just like that, the crow fell from the wire and spiraled to the ground.

And when going downtown, Walter says, gesturing with his hands, *take the #9, except late at night, when you should take the #2 and transfer to the #4. And sometimes, short catnaps can be just as good as long, uninterrupted sleep . . .*

At the hospital, in the hallway, doctors and nurses hold their stethoscopes to their chests to keep them from bouncing as they rush toward an emergency. On the television, a man gets yet another pie in the face.

The Visiting Dignitary half-sleeps crookedly in his easy chair, muttering, *But I want I want I want . . .*

The crow lay on its side and flexed its talons. Already crying, the Zoo Director scooped the crow from the ground and ran into the house, screaming.

What have I done? he cried as he held the stiffening crow out to his mother. She took the crow and placed it on the table and told her son to touch the crow and give it ease as it passed.

We are defined by our mercy, she told her son.

As the crow died, the Zoo Director stroked its black wing while his mother wiped the tears from his eyes with a dishtowel.

It would be wrong to say, necessarily, that the Zoo Director thinks of this incident as the 10:21 moves toward him, because it happened so long ago, but even so, as a soft beep indicates the target is in range, the Zoo Director drops the launcher from his shoulder and moves the safety back to on.

Before doing anything, turn off the circuit-breaker and attach the ground, Jane tells the penguin. *Beware of compound interest loans and strangers bearing gifts. Measure twice to cut once.*

To all this, Walter nods as his love reaches forth and seals the three of them—Jane, the penguin, himself—in its grip. He signals the waitress for another round of cocoa, and perhaps they could share just a taste of the cream pie too.

Finished with, the Zoo Custodian looks both ways before raising his arms and jogging toward the uncut red ribbon. As he runs through the tape, the Zoo Custodian blows kisses to the imaginary crowd. His ears ring with cheering.

At the hospital, the child shifts in sleep and groans softly from the pain of the broken arm. Tomorrow he will have surgery; they will insert screws and pins for the bones to grow around to repair the damage. At school, he will show his arm to the other children and chop the air and claim superpowers. But for now the child turns and drapes his good arm across his mother and touches his fingers at her forehead in a gesture of blessing.

What I Am, What I Found, What I Did

(Attachments Enclosed)

It is important that certain things be cleared up. What I did was not a protest, and I am not nor ever have been affiliated with any anti-government, citizen militia group. I am not an Islamist or anything like that. I'm not entirely sure what an Islamist is. What I did should not—and I cannot emphasize this enough—be compared to the tragedy at Oklahoma City or, God forbid, the attacks on 9/11. I am not a gun-and-explosive-toting madman seeking to overthrow Western civilization. What I am is an economist.

I have a B.A. from Rice and a Ph.D. from the University of Chicago. My studies surrounding what I did were sound in concept and executed with the utmost thoroughness, as befits my background and experience. I have been cataloguing the economic health of Lake Charles, Louisiana, for close to eleven years now, which is to say I did what I did only after much difficult deliberation. Economics is a science, and it was with this in mind that I finally decided to do what I did. If there were another way to achieve the desired result, I would have found it. But there was no other way; the numbers simply don't lie. And while a few casualties were necessary for the ultimate success of the project, I deeply regret there were so many.

Six hundred forty-two people injured is a most unfortunate number, but I think it's important to remember—now that the forensic report on Mr. James T. May indicates that he had suffered a fatal myocardial infarction prior to the first explosion—that my actions resulted in no deaths. I also maintain that many of these injuries could have been avoided if the crew did not panic. Let's face it, the boat was sinking very, very slowly. Because of the crew's slipshod service, I have drafted a letter to Congress (Attachment 1), urging them to examine the training programs, if indeed there are any in place for these people. Yes, their primary jobs are to deal blackjack and schlep watered-down drinks to customers flushing their final pennies down a bottomless well of stupidity, but let's remember, this is all happening upon a ship in navigable waters. Rather than training their attention on the engine of capitalism, our financial services industry, perhaps our government regulators should look this-a-ways. In addition, contrary to published reports, my actions were not predicated on a grudge against Mr. Merv Griffin or his legacy. I did, in fact, very much enjoy his television show when it was a daytime staple. And while I am a Christian and believe gambling to be a sin, I am also a pragmatist; therefore I am the first to acknowledge the beneficial effect that Mr. Merv Griffin and his consortium have had on the greater Lake Charles area with the introduction of their riverboat casinos.

Bringing gambling to Lake Charles lowered unemployment, increased the tax base, raised the number of housing starts, and stimulated the regeneration of a downtown nearly destroyed by the invasion of the Walmart out on Highway 14 (Attachments 2–5. Also, see my article in the June issue of the *Journal of Business and Economics,* "Here Comes Walmart, There Goes the Neighborhood").

However, as has been well established, we are in the midst of a historically bad economic downturn, and the numbers make it clear that we are in dire need of additional economic stimulus in order to maintain a viable and at least semi-prosperous community (Attachment 6). If you'll pardon the metaphor, in the current competition for the discretionary dollar, Lake Charles is armed with a slingshot in an automatic-weapons world.

As a staunch believer that free markets make free people, I felt it was both impractical and immoral to turn to government to bail us out. If loving Ayn Rand is wrong, I don't want to be right, and so I resolved to go Galt on behalf of the Interstate 10 corridor between Vinton and Lafayette.

The key to meeting the challenges of a twenty-first-century economy was to transition Lake Charles from a semi-failed postindustrial city known for its chemical processing plants into a tourist paradise. After some initial investigations, it became clear that Hawaii was the perfect model.

I have never been to Hawaii, though I have seen it on TV shows such as *Magnum P.I.*, and that one episode of *The Brady Bunch*, as well as in films such as *Blue Crush* and *Lilo and Stitch*. By all accounts it is a lovely place. And while *I* have not been to Hawaii, many others have, which is reflected in the fact that Hawaii derives more of its income from tourism than any other state in the union (Attachment 7). There are, in fact, many, many things to do in Hawaii (Attachment 8): swim, surf, helicopter rides, parasailing, hiking, volcano tours, luaus, along with all kinds of other things I can't think of right now, and with all these different activities, you would think no solid, single theory as to the incredible lure of Hawaii could be formulated, but my findings were most surprising and quite conclusive.

What I found was that people simply love shipwrecks. Even with the countless numbers of tourist activities available on the five Hawaiian islands, the number-eleven-most favorite attraction is the memorial to the USS *Arizona* (Attachment 9). Thanks to the cooperation of Witherspoon Travel Partners Worldwide (Attachment 10), I was able to interview, by phone, nearly one dozen people who had taken recent trips to Hawaii, and time and again I found the *Arizona* popping up as a highlight (Attachment 11). Even though most of the people had only a limited understanding of the history surrounding the *Arizona*, across the board the respondents thought the experience of visiting a shipwreck was "pretty neat," and the idea that people had died there, on that very spot, "cool," or "creepy, but still totally cool" (Attachment 12). If we need further proof than this, all I have to say is that I trust that I'm not the only one here who remembers a little something called the *Titanic*.

Thus it became clear to me that what Lake Charles needed was a shipwreck of its own, so this is what I did: I decided to sink the *Star* riverboat casino owned by Merv Griffin Enterprises and its consortium of investors. I chose the *Star* because of two factors: (1) It was the oldest of the three riverboats operating on Lake Charles, making it most likely the first to be replaced anyway, and (2) since Merv Griffin Enterprises and his consortium also operate the *Players* riverboat casino, I figured it was only fair, rather than sinking the competing Isle of Capri's only casino riverboat and therefore putting them out of business and reducing competition.

On April 16, I officially hired Mitchell Patchett for the sum of three thousand dollars after contacting him at the number included in his advertisement in the back of *Soldier of Fortune* magazine (Attachment 13). He told me he was an ex–Navy Seal, skilled in underwater operations and explosives. This, as we all know now, was most definitely true. Indeed, it was clear that Mitchell Patchett was skilled in all manner of "field ops," and the things he could do with a serrated-edge "kill" knife were simply amazing. However, at no time did he tell me about his psychiatric discharge from the military, or his subsequent three-year hospital stay. If I regret any of my actions, it is that I did not check Mitchell Patchett's background more thoroughly.

We trained six weeks for the operation. I became versed in all aspects of commando stealth maneuvers under the direction of Mitchell Patchett, who was especially fond of barking orders. Even though they were not part of our plan, I learned how to field-strip an M-16 rifle and disarm a "hot" Claymore. As an example of the prowess I gained, I now have sufficient grip strength to pop a tennis ball in my hand. If one needs further proof, I suggest s/he review the autopsy report of my former cellmate Lonnie "The Cutter" Watkins (Attachment 14).

The night of the operation was perfect, moonless and clear with almost no chop. Mitchell Patchett and I thought we had slipped into the water unseen, but postaction, eyewitness reports from Donald and Noreen Taylor (Attachment 15), who were apparently enjoying a lakefront stroll, indicate this was not true. The swim to the *Star* was not strenuous, but we found the hull grime-covered and slick (a further indication, I believe, of a lax crew), so only after some quick but vigorous scrubbing were we able to attach the C-4 explosive packages and their Herman A-1 detonators to the ship without being detected. Upon finishing this task, Mitchell Patchett thumped his fist on the side of the hull twice before giving me the thumbs up. "It's gonna be a beaut," he said. I circled my finger in the air once quickly before pointing down to the water in the appropriate gesture to indicate that we had a "go" mission.

As planned, Mitchell Patchett and I were back on shore at the time of detonation. When the C-4 exploded, it blew a ("good sized," according to the NTSB report) hole in the side and the *Star* began clearly listing to starboard (Attachment 16). A small fire could be seen emanating from the wound, the flames licking over the side. From our position, Mitchell Patchett and I could obviously not see what was happening onboard, but we could hear it. Newspaper reports have described the ensuing scene as "panic," but this seems to be yet another example of media sensationalism as, quite honestly, it sounded much closer to excitement than panic, an impression borne out by two additional pieces of evidence documented in Appendixes B (Attachment 17) and C (Attachment 18) to the after-action report. First, as Appendix B makes clear, most of the documented injuries are human-inflicted scratches, gouges, and bites. This, combined with the fact that nearly 2.3 million dollars' worth of casino chips are unaccounted for following the full search and salvage operation, suggests that, postdetonation, the passengers' attention might have been on something other than mere survival. Let me also note that not a single one of them has so much as hinted at a civil suit against me.

I couldn't have asked much more from the actual sinking. The *Star*'s lighted neon sign exploding like Fourth of July fireworks just prior to the final submerging was an unexpectedly poetic bonus. I suppose I would have preferred a more majestic descent to the bottom— stern first, with bow pointed skyward—but the *Star* flopping on its side like it was exhausted and needed a rest is perhaps a more appropriate symbol for our times.

There isn't much else, I suppose. I remember the sirens, the people bobbing in the water individually and in lifeboats, shouting to each other, "How much ya get?" After a while, I noticed that Mitchell Patchett was cackling. He held his hands at his waist and rocked back and forth and simply laughed and laughed like he wouldn't stop. I looked into his eyes and saw the final sparks from the exploding sign dancing on his pupils and behind those sparks I saw nothing, absolutely not a single thing, and while I admit that he is most likely deranged, I maintain that he is not insane (as his attorney is making him out to be), that he knew and knows right from wrong like anyone else, and thus I urge the courts to "throw the book at him" (see "Book" as Attachment 19). Once the ship sank entirely beneath the surface, thus extinguishing the orange glow of the fire, the night's only source of light, I never saw Mitchell Patchett again, though I was relieved to hear of his apprehension. Clearly, he is a most dangerous man.

My capture and arrest are a matter of public record, personal humiliation, and extreme vilification at the hands of the news media. I can only urge the people of America to take into account what I have to say here when it comes to making up their minds about me. While others have dithered, I acted, and for that, it's hard to apologize.

However, because my lawyer says I should, I would also like to take this opportunity to personally express regret to each and every injured passenger (Attachments 20–670), even if they don't necessarily deserve it, and lastly, try to get a message to my wife, Betty, since the phone is always busy and for some reason my letters (Attachments

671–819) have all been returned unopened. To Betty I say: I love you, honey, and I know we'll beat this.

Finally, a word of caution to other economists. As I was running from the police pursuit as fast as my flippered feet would allow, their shouts of "get the FUCK DOWN you GODDAMN MOTHER-FUCKER!" ringing in my ears as the shots fired just over my head whistled past, I remembered something I'd learned in Economics 101, something that maybe I'd forgotten, but something I hope all economists will forever keep in mind from now on. While economics may be the most beautiful, the most wondrous, of our *theoretical* sciences, it is important to remember that the application of any theory, no matter how sound its base, can be considerably more complex than one might have thought.

Poet Farmers

Ruthie saw them first. She shaded her eyes with a hand and pointed at a group kicking up dust along the drive. Capes flapped behind as they walked, and each one of them clutched a wire notebook and pen. "Shit damn," Ruthie said to Roy. "Looks like we got poets."

The leader, pale and pointy-nosed, scooped up a handful of dirt and breathed it in deeply before dumping it inside the folds of his cape. "Show us your world; there is poetry here," he said as the others muttered and surrounded Ruthie, gauging her thighs.

"Like oak," one said.

"No, granite," offered another, and it looked like there was going to be a dust-up over which word was right, until one got too close and Ruthie slapped a grabbing hand from the hem of her dress.

"Well, Roy, I guess you should show 'em what they're after," she said.

The poets' capes gently swayed, windless and limp, as they stalked the new John Deere. One frowned as he picked at the hard enamel paint while others climbed into the cab and shuddered from the blare of Hank Jr. on the CD player. Roy showed them the cool ease of the power steering, the air-conditioning, and the fully electronic, adjustable seat. When Roy cranked the engine, the poets scattered from the pistons' howl.

"Bunch o' hens," Roy spat. He thought for a moment that he might've gotten rid of those poets, but as he headed back toward the house, he heard the murmur of their capes as they regrouped behind him.

Ruthie sat them around the kitchen for some of her countywide-famous black-raspberry tarts and naturally sweetened ice tea, but there was nary a nibble or sip, and it looked for a while like those poets were about ready to move on until one of them spied the weathered planks of the old barn.

"Over there!" he shouted.

As they ran toward the barn they bellowed, "Show us the cracked hide of old mule straps and the blunted blade of the once-keen plow! Show us the toil and the drought, the struggle against soil! Show us poetry!" Ruthie looked at Roy and Roy looked at Ruthie and they both shrugged, but they were glad for their once again empty kitchen, and so they let the poets pore over those rusty things.

After a couple months some left, notebooks bulging, but still more came seeking their muse. They were, for sure, a nuisance. Ruthie and Roy considered their alternatives: a good herbicide, the National Guard, or some local toughs brought round after one too many, maybe, but nothing seemed quite right until one night, Ruthie and Roy had this conversation:

"Roy?"

"Yeah?"

"You remember our dream, Roy?"

"Oh yeah."

"The Princess Royal Ultra Luxury Cruise Line, twelve days and eleven nights, nights that are preceded by dazzling sunsets and end with us exhausted from dancing, drinking, and good cheer. You remember that, right, Roy?"

"Twenty-four-hour-a-day cabin boys named Hector or Lars, honey."

"You remember what it said the poolside drinks tasted like, Roy?"

"I believe it was nectar. Sun-drenched nectar, topped with honey, honey."

At this point Ruthie paused for a moment as she ran her hand down Roy's arm and made every single hair on his whole body stand straight up. Roy marveled at how Ruthie could do that even after their many years of marriage.

"We're farmers, aren't we, Roy?"

"Oh yeah, we're farmers all right."

"And the beans, Roy?"

"Bad year for beans, Ruthie."

Ruthie smiled, smiled more seductively than you might imagine, and said, "Well, I know something we got too much of, Roy." And that night Roy surely did enjoy Ruthie's iron thighs.

They had acres of poets buried navel deep. Rows and rows of them always stocked with notebooks and pens and kept fat on fried chicken, squash, whole milk, and Mars bars. Nights, while Ruthie and Roy dreamed of Caribbean vistas, those poets slept, covered with their capes.

But the first crop was no good—bad enjambment, thoughtless stanza breaks, and clichés crept across them like blight—and Roy and Ruthie were about to give up on poets as a problem they could not crack, and with it their lifelong dream of cruising the Caribbean, but then they had another conversation:

"Roy?"

"Yeah, honey?"

"You remember what Wittgenstein used to say, Roy?"

"Seems to me he said a lot of things."

"What I'm thinking of is this particular thing, and you stop me if I'm wrong, Roy: 'The riddle does not exist. If a question can be put at all, then it can also be answered.'"

"You're not wrong, honey. Now why don't you stop fiddling with that poetry nonsense and come over here so we can share our love?"

And that night Ruthie did as she was asked, gladly.

So they switched the poets to a diet of citrus fruits, bean sprouts, the occasional organ meat or lean veal cutlet with a dry, white sherry for a nightcap, and soon enough the yield started getting better.

Roy gathered the sheets of paper from the fields and rubbed Ruthie's shoulders as she typed them up, polished the metaphors and fixed some other rough spots:

"You remember what else Wittgenstein said, Roy?"

"Are you thinking of, 'Everything that can be said can be said clearly,' honey?"

"I am, Roy."

"I clearly love you, my sweet, sweet Ruthie Ann," Roy said.

And soon enough they had a bumper crop and a real New York agent named Silverberg, and the critics almost tripped over their tongues, they were so fat with praise. Just last week, Silverberg gave Ruthie and Roy the word that they'd won an honest-to-goodness Pulitzer Prize. A Pulitzer Prize! A Pulitzer Prize, which even Roy and Ruthie know is a pretty big deal. So Ruthie went off cape-shopping to prepare for a full twelve days and eleven nights of leaving all cares behind, while Roy, Roy is checking with Ted from next door to see if he'll take a few stray sonnets as pay to look after the fields while Roy and Ruthie cruise.

And while Ted believes in being neighborly, he's still thinking that he'll have to hold out for a suite of sestinas, perhaps about the rain and how it sounds when it strikes the roofs of farmhouses, old tin barns, or waving blades of field grass.

Tough Day for the Army

The army waits, nerve-jangled, for the word.

Waiting, the army sits, awkward and uncomfortable on the molded orange plastic waiting room chairs. The chairs offer little cover from ambush or sniper. In normal times (which these are not, but when are they ever?), the army would never willingly choose this location.

Forward scouts were dispatched long ago to the window by the counter (behind which the bun-haired woman sits) to retrieve word, and they are much overdue.

The army thinks a little air support might be nice, just in case, a little softening up: of a couple thousand tons of high explosive, maybe a dash of incendiary, clear some clutter, strategic-like, surgical. Drones. Predator drones. Hellfire. Air support, despite the noise, the chaos, the debris, despite its origination in a rival branch of the service, has always been oddly comforting to the army. In times past, as the concussion from the air support bombs would wash over them, the army would think: *Take that, suckers. Bet you didn't bargain for that, suckers. You are dead dead and dead, suckers. Suckers.*

But their radios broadcast only static now. They know it is possible (probable?) that headquarters has been compromised, but they soldier on because this is what soldiers do.

Perched on the tiny, scooped-out chairs, the army is clumsy in its bulging packs, dangling entrenching tools, and various weapons. The army tries to be as silent as possible, but this is, in reality, not silent at all. Truth be told, the army makes a racket. Their boots are thick and hard at the soles—with the slightest twitch, the leather and Gore-Tex creaks unagreeably around the ankle—and because of an excess of design, ingenuity, and Yankee know-how, the average infantryman is way overloaded, poundage-wise, with "necessary" gear. (Note: In battle, when the deadly exchange of flying metal commences, it is well known that pretty much only the rifle is necessary. Maybe the helmet just a little, in case of glancing shrapnel, but mostly just the rifle, and yes, the helmet if possible, but only if possible, let's call it an extra, a bonus.)

Other guests of the waiting room stare as the army accidentally knocks stacks of old magazines from end table to floor. Carefully, the army picks up the magazines, restacks them, then casually, very casually, so as not to attract attention, leafs through one and rips out colorful recipes that look suitable for cooking over Sterno.

An old woman says: Those are old, the magazines. There's newer ones somewhere. The receptionist hides them. It's like a game to her.

The army thanks the woman kindly for that advice and asks if she thinks the pictures accompanying the recipes look good. Don't they look good? the army says.

The woman shakes her head, smiles ruefully, says: Sure, of course the pictures look good, real good, good enough to eat, ha ha ha, but they don't look like that when you cook them. Don't look like that at all, no sirs. If you ate the actual objects that were used in the composition and creation of that photograph, you'd be . . . well I sure wouldn't want to . . . what I'm trying to say is . . . pain . . . you'd experience some pain for sure, explosive pain even. We're talking toilet hugging for sure kind of pain, maybe . . . who knows? Worse? Hospital pain, real gurney-clutching, tear-your-own-heart-out, tunnel-vision-blackout kind of pain. You see what I'm getting at?

The army nods in the affirmative. Armies know of these things, these things and worse.

The woman says: That picture there is what's known as professional food photography, wherein you substitute the food with something that looks more foodlike when photographed in two dimensions under controlled lighting conditions. The niblet corn is really spray-painted rubber and that there asparagus is made out of retired fake Christmas trees dragged out of dumpsters. The chicken is old eraser bits molded under precise heat and rubbed shiny and golden with dandelion extract, which is a well-known technique for these cases. I'm surprised you haven't heard of this.

We've been away, busy, the army says, casting shame-filled eyes downward.

I just hate to see such nice boys fooled is all. It's all a trick, you see. Sometimes now they use computers too. The idea is that one thing becomes another; then it's not lying.

The army nods, sees its hulking reflection in the office glass, and thinks that, tactically speaking, this could all be a mistake.

But what choice?

Near the receptionist's desk, the forward scouts softly clear their throats and tap their fingers near the dried-up pen permanently chained to the counter, but the receptionist remains glassy-eyed and unmoved.

Amongst the army, Lumpkins clicks open the bolt on his carbine, removes the bolt, eyes down the barrel, clicks the bolt shut again, clicks open, removes, eyes down, shut again, says to Henderson: What do you think the word's gonna be?

Word's never good, Lump. Never.

Maybe today?

Nope. Never.

Let me tell you, I once had a sister. She was so pretty that. . .

We all did, Lump. Get in line. Take a number. Get over it.

This is an army's life, hurry up and wait.

Lumpkins works his poem:

I once had a sister
She was so pretty that . . .

. . . but can't get any further. Words fail, frequently.

At least, in times past, I've done some pretty fine talking with my gun, Lumpkins thinks:

Ratta-tatta-tat,
Take that.

The army worries about the forms. They filled them in as best they could, smiled as they were handed to the receptionist, but it is always hard to know what might be appropriate, what, precisely, they are looking for. Under the heading for "Competencies" they recorded the following:

I guess you could say that mostly, we're an ultra-efficient killing machine. We have our problems, our inevitable shortcomings, sure, but we're probably the greatest killing machine the world has ever known, although this is tough to say (meaning difficult to gauge) since we've been overstretched, occasionally misused, and, in recent times, have mostly taken on the backwards and overmatched, who believe in asymmetrical warfare, which isn't as interesting as it sounds, and mostly involves trying to blow us up with shit buried in the ground because they know face to face, they would reap the whirlwind since they have no chance against a gun-type instrument wielded by a soldier trained to a razor-fine peak of physical and mental fitness. In any hands, untrained hands even, these gun-type instruments are deadly, very much so deadly. When you're talking the combination of deadly instruments and a force (Again, physically and mentally quite, quite primed; this cannot be stressed enough) that is ready/willing/able to use said instruments for their designed purpose (And let's not mince words, that purpose would be killing), well, and you must agree, you've got something pretty potent happening there.

Meaning, we are not something you would like to mess with. Sure, if you had a time machine and you sent us back to face, for example, the Huns, or better yet, the Mongol Horde, on their own turf, well that might just be a tough bitch to crack—we sure as hell wouldn't go down without a fight, though, you can bet on that, last man standing etcetera, etcetera . . . But you bring the Horde here, to our present-day reality, you bring them here, invite them inside our house of pain, and by the time they finished rubbing the surprise from their eyes and said the shortest prayer possible to whatever it is those godless fucks hold dear, we would give them a serious stomping. We would wrap up those stinky, inbred, slant-eyed motherfuckers in a shit storm of truly biblical proportions, real Book-of-Revelations-Wrath-of-God shit rained down upon them, by us, because we are more than qualified (eager even) to do so. All that aside and everything taken into account, ergo, it is more than fair to say that as of this moment, we can't be touched in terms of killing.

The response went well past the five or so crowded lines provided on the form, lines that would be insufficient for any answer, let alone one as complete as the army's. This meant the army had to write in the margins and on the reverse, and use arrows and write "over" and "cont." and all manner of things, and the army felt as though their warning sensors detected a scowl cross the face of the bun-haired sentinel when they slid the finished product through the slot, beneath the protective glass.

Eventually the forward scouts return, heads hanging, sans word. They say the word will come when it is ready, in essence, when there is word, but as of now, no word. Who knows when? They don't, *so stop asking.*

This is the soldier's life, hurry up, then wait. Mostly wait . . . wait . . . wait . . . wait . . .

Do you remember? Lumpkins asks Henderson.

Yes, says Henderson.

Do you remember when we were on that mission in the faraway country where there were the skinny brown men with the stained teeth from the betel nuts who carried their antiquated and slow-loading rifles beneath unbuttoned cloth shirts that billowed behind them as they charged toward us, heedless of our ability to cut them down with well-placed volleys of withering fire delivered from strategic vantage points that maximized the shooting field, but at the same time minimized the danger of injury or death due to friendly fire?

Yes, I remember. We were fighting in the streets to establish order and subsequently to banish the feudal warlords and install the properly organized democratic government. Also to provide food to the hungry of whom there were very, very many. Those men that charged at us held bullets in their teeth so they could reload as quickly as possible. The bullets looked like metal fangs. On the other hand, we could reload by changing ammo clips in approximately 1.6 seconds.

Do you remember how the men sometimes, as they charged toward us, shielded themselves with children, thinking that we would not shoot children? Lumpkins says.

Yes, Henderson says.

It's fortunate that we are such good shots that we were able to shoot the men but avoid harming the children, Lumpkins says.

What were we supposed to do? They were trying to kill us, after all, which despite the practice and training we'd endured was sort of surprising, how much they could want to kill us, Henderson says.

And do you remember the special rounds we used that were designed to go through armor but had the unfortunate effect of passing *too* cleanly through their human bodies and thus failed to knock these charging men down upon impact as more traditional small arms ordnance does, and how the men, clutching the small children, would continue to advance even as they were shot again and again and again?

Yes. I remember the same way you do. I remember terribly and often.

Do you remember the liberation? The time we went to give them their rights as declared by God and the United States of America and they kept trying to blow us up?

Yes, they hated us too.

I didn't hate them.

It wasn't our fault, or theirs.

Do you remember how I carried that old Royal typewriter everywhere, how I would bang out paragraphs of memories even as they happened, how once, as I crouched behind an overturned car, getting something down, that old Royal deflected a bullet destined to deliver a mortal wound and lost only the use of the nearly nonessential X key in the process?

Yes, yes, and I had the old transistor radio with foil wrapped around the antenna that we would set up in barracks and dance to rhythm-and-blues music and get high and share good times as our smooth-muscled torsos flashed with sweat and . . .

In the waiting room, as the varying people wait for their varying reasons, wait for their varying orders to send them into the various recesses of the building (or beyond), wait to be hurled to their varying fates, throats are cleared, sideways glances exchanged, legs crossed and uncrossed, foreign bits are surreptitiously picked from teeth while no one (in reality, though, everyone) is looking. A child grips an empty plastic cup in one hand, and with the other rubs the corner of the cardboard cover of a worn-out picture book, peels the layers until the cardboard is frayed and soft as tissue. The child lifts the book to his face and sniffs between the paper layers, thinks: *no one has smelled this before. No one but me.*

The army wonders if it should amend the answer on the form and mention the looting prevention, the quelling of the garden-variety civil unrest, or the dam-building, how they deliver food and supplies to the poor and war-ravaged. These are the peace missions, but of course even the fighting missions are *in the interests of peace* meaning that they are there to establish peace where there is none, working as the handmaiden of peace, if you will, a peace forged out of their irresistible might. Does that seem contradictory?

A slash of light on the carpet disappears as the sun moves behind a more impressive building outside.

Henderson thinks: *Maybe a warning shot. Just to juice things up.* But does nothing, just like the rest.

Lumpkins tries his poem again

I once had
a sister.
She was
so pretty
that I could
have . . .

Tired of waiting, the child throws the book down and totters across the floor, banging its hand over its mouth, whooping like an Indian.

Finally the receptionist looks up, and it is clear, the word is here. The whole room sits at the edge of their seats. Breaths are held.

Something is coming, and it's heading this way.

A Love Story

"How long?"

"Excuse me?

"How long have you loved her?"

I was almost always the last out the door of Señora Nuborgen's Spanish class. My last name, Zimmerman, kept me pinned in back of the alphabetically ordered rows, and I also spent most of every class daydreaming, or sometimes sleeping, and was always a beat behind when it came time to leave, at least compared to my clock-watching classmates, who looked spring-loaded when the bell rang. We were in the second-to-last week of school, the last period of the day, mostly seniors, which meant we'd all had enough, Señora Nuborgen included, which meant movie week, which meant we were watching a mid-'60s West German production of *Don Quixote*. It was some kind of miniseries, dubbed from German into Spanish and then subtitled into English, and for most of us it was instant Sominex. The more popular versions must have been claimed by other schools out of the regional district A/V library. Señora Nuborgen often seemed a beat behind herself that semester. The circles under her eyes had darkened. Her clothes hung loose and shapeless. Sometimes she seemed to be leaning on the desk for support.

I looked at my shoes and then at the books cradled in my hand. I still carried them around as a prop, even though I had no use for them. "No sé," I said. Señora Nuborgen insisted that we speak Spanish at all times during class.

"You don't know?"

"What? No! I meant no comprende."

"What don't you understand?" Señora Nuborgen looked at me from behind her desk, both hands placed flat against her grade book. She wore what she always wore, a button-up sweater over a frilly blouse, an endless combination of argyles and creams. Her skirt, mid-calf length, must have been either gray or black or brown, and the pantyhose in that color that only teachers wear. I suppose the package would have been labeled "flesh," though no human has that skin tone. If you asked me how old she was I'm sure my seventeen-year-old self would have said "like fifty?" but she was probably in her mid- to late thirties, or about the age I am now.

"No estas en amor," I said, wondering why *she* wasn't speaking Spanish, but I figured sticking with it gave me some plausible deniability as to what we were talking about.

Señora Nuborgen sighed and tapped her fingers softly over the grade book like she was picking out notes on a piano. "*Estoy,* not *estas. No estoy en amor.* I am not in love. You said to me, 'You are not in love,' which is true enough, but not what you meant."

"No comprende?"

"No, I suppose you don't," she said. She lowered her head, like she was praying over the grade book. I knew you weren't supposed to walk away from a teacher until they were done talking to you, but I eased out the door before she could look up again.

I haven't thought of Jennifer Mecklenberg in a long time, years, not until the other night in bed, when my wife turned toward me and placed her hand on the book I was reading, lowering it from my gaze so I would look at her. Her face was sleepy, in that last moment of evening consciousness. "Do you love me?" she said.

"Of course."

"Don't answer that way," she replied. Her blinks were slow and heavy.

"What way?" I said, lifting the book back up, but still looking at her.

"Unthinking, like it's some sort of reflex."

"Why can't my love for you be a reflex?"

Her eyes closed fully.

"Because that's not how love is," she said softly, almost sighing. She breathed deeply, slowly, asleep. I turned back to my book.

"I know I'm not the only one you've loved," she said. Her eyes were still closed, her voice a whisper, like she was talking to herself. I lowered my book again.

"You're the only one I've ever *really* loved," I said. I placed a hand on her shoulder then slid it to her rising and falling ribs.

She didn't reply for a while, and then she spoke again. "You know that's not true."

She could have been talking in her sleep, for all I could figure. Her face was slack, the fine wrinkles that have started to appear around her eyes smoothed away. I went back to my book, but my eyes just ran over the words, taking nothing in. I turned off the light and settled in next to her. Beth slung a leg and arm over me and nuzzled into my neck. "You're not off the hook," she said, close, into my ear. "I'll expect a better answer next time I ask."

And so I've been thinking about love, which brought me back to Jennifer Mecklenberg and Señora Nuborgen. I actually comprended what Señora Nuborgen was saying *muy bien* or *mucho bien,* or whatever. I had loved Jennifer Mecklenberg unrequitedly for better than two years at that point. All through high school we'd been in the same classes, parallel lines that never intersected because since even before I'd loved her she had an older boyfriend, Andrew Collins, the son of an airline CEO, the kind of kid who was loud in the hallways, tall, broad-shouldered, confident and showy. He had matured, and I had not. He would come up behind her in the halls and grab her shoulders and give her a little shake. "Jenny Meck!" he'd shout, turning her to face him, staking his claim. He was the only person I'd ever heard call her "Jenny," and whenever he said this, I swear I saw her cringe a little. She was not a Jenny. Maybe a "Jen" to her girlfriends, but a Jennifer to the rest of us.

I remember her as beautiful, but when I dug out my senior yearbook recently, the picture I found showed a girl who was merely pretty, with brown, shoulder-length hair, a string of pearls over her navy sweater and white turtleneck. I didn't remember the braces, but there they were. I couldn't imagine that Jennifer Mecklenberg still had braces senior year. Even I'd managed to shed them by October. I turned to my own picture, looking sidelong at the wiry hair sculpted into a helmet just long enough for a single snap. I couldn't bear to look long enough to decide if I really was as out of her league as I felt at the time. I ask myself why I loved her, and I honestly don't know. I didn't even really know her—my biggest success wooing her was in a group project in European History the previous year, when I'd made some crack and she playfully punched me in the arm, saying, "You're so funny!" which was something, but not very much.

But as I remember her, the feeling returns, not with its full force, but stronger than I'd think it should or could, having been blunted by twenty years.

I could go to Facebook, but this requires exposure, and Beth would see, and there is something about making it a detective game that appeals to me. Class reunion websites are a treasure trove of information. Some of the profiles are free to peruse and I spent hours virtually catching up with my former classmates. Julie Vandenbosch is deceased, killed by a drunk driver. Marcy Bobcheck is now Mark Bobcheck. (Neither I nor her former softball teammates should be surprised.) Richard Pendarvis made a fortune in dot coms and apparently exclusively wears Hawaiian shirts. Most everyone is or at least has been married. Many are bald or balding. All these factoids are both surprising and not. Who would have figured that Tim Penn would be arrested for allegedly spying on his fifteen-year-old neighbor with a remote video camera planted in her room? But then again, it sort of makes sense if you knew him back in the day.

She is on one of the websites as Jennifer Mecklenberg Schmitz, but her information is labeled as "private," and the icons next to her name indicate that she has posted a full biography and pictures available for anyone willing to pony up the $19.95 annual fee. I wouldn't know how to explain the charge to my wife.

I googled her name and read tidbits about at least twelve different Jennifer Schmitzes, all of whom or none of whom could be her. She could be the leading real estate salesperson of Greensboro, North Carolina, or someone concerned about faulty playground equipment on the tot lots in Dowagiac, Michigan. She may not be either of these people. She's probably not both.

There are bulletin boards on these sites where we are told to post our most memorable moments and then others can comment on them. I scroll through the list, and I remember none of those posted by others, but then again no one would remember mine, either.

The next day in Señora Nuborgen's class I stayed alert to the clock, ready to jump into the middle of the line filing so as not to be cornered again, but a minute or so before the bell was due to ring, just as Quixote convinced Sancho Panza to be his squire, Señora Nuborgen clicked on the lights, saying, "That's a good stopping point. Have a good weekend, everyone. We'll finish up next week. Remember that attendance matters, and Josh Z., I need to speak to you for a moment."

When the bell rang I stayed seated at my desk. Señora Nuborgen and I were alone inside thirty seconds, the student stampede over, leaving rows of crooked desks in its wake. She advanced from the front of the room and grabbed a nearby seat, turning it to face me.

I fumbled for the right words. "Que hice mal?"

She smiled. "Very good. You said that correctly. You haven't done anything wrong, at least in regards to class."

I went to my go-to phrase, "No comprende."

"Back to that, are we? You can drop the Spanish bullshit. It's sort of painful for us both, and you're not going to remember any of this by the time you start college in the fall anyway."

I swallowed hard. I don't remember being scared, more like unsettled. Teachers were not supposed to speak to students like this and the party line for four years had been that everything was important because we'd have to know it for college. Señora Nuborgen looked at me steadily, blocking my exit with her desk. I would've had to literally leap over her to get out. "Why am I here?" I said.

"You never answered my question from yesterday."

"What question?"

"How long have you loved her?"

"Who?"

"Don't play dumb, Josh," she said, sitting heavily back in the desk. "I've been teaching here thirteen years and during that time I've seen a lot of love on the faces of you kids. I've seen the look someone has when they're in love, and I see it on your face when you look at Jennifer Mecklenberg. I don't blame you, she's cute, but then everyone's cute at your age."

At the sound of her name, my heart filliped against my chest.

"Aha!" Señora Nuborgen said, sitting up straight and slapping the desk. "There it was again. I knew it. So, how long?"

There was something kind in her eyes, so I decided to tell as much truth as I could stand. "I dunno, a while."

"A while, huh?"

"Yeah."

"What's a while?"

"A couple of years, maybe?"

"I bet that feels like a long time," she said. She angled her head a little, looking at me more closely.

I said nothing, and Señora Nuborgen looked away and then up at the ceiling, like she might find more questions there. "Have you been enjoying the movie?" she said.

"Sure."

"Liar." She smiled briefly at me before looking back at the ceiling. "Do you know what *Don Quixote* is about?"

I'd read the Cliffs Notes like everyone else. "I dunno, some crazy guy?" I said.

"You kids always phrase your answers as questions, not that I blame you. I wasn't sure if I knew anything at your age either, but you know more than you think, believe me. Some crazy guy, huh? I suppose that's right." She gripped the desk and pulled herself back upright, leaning across the desk's surface and toward me. "Do you know what I think it's about?"

"What?"

"Doing what you think is right, even if it's wrong."

She gave her biggest smile of the afternoon, but I must have been looking at her like she was Don Quixote because it quickly fell. She lowered her head to the desk and rested it across her folded arms. "You can go now, if you want," she said into the crook of her elbow. The sound of the squeaking chair echoed around the room as I stood. I moved quietly as I could to the door, holding my breath. At the threshold I glanced back to see her still with her head down, unmoving.

I've been doing most of my thinking about love during my "runs." I am not a natural runner, but I have reached the age where activity is a near daily necessity if I want to live a life of a reasonable duration. The first ten or so minutes of each session involve a cataloguing of that day's aches and pains—the creaking in my arthritic big toe, the shooting sensation down the inside of my left arm that I've come to ignore because it is apparently not a heart attack, the tightening cramp in the upper right abdominal. In order to escape this litany I make an effort to think about anything else, and lately I've been thinking about why my wife might be thinking about love.

Maybe it is because we recently acknowledged that it is very likely that we will not be having children. We are not too old, but we are getting there, and if the window of opportunity feels like it is not shut completely, it is at most cracked, and as it closes, neither of us feels any real urgency to wedge it open. We have agreed that while our home is perhaps a hospitable place for a child, the world, increasingly, is not. This seals our fates only to each other. This is a scary thought for sure, but as creaky as I feel some days, it seems distant enough that it doesn't cause me any particular worry. It is something inevitable, and maybe not even for me since I will likely be the first to go.

To me, what we have together feels complete enough for this lifetime; at least that's my sense of things and has been from just about the moment we met. Truthfully, I'm not sure about Beth's. You'd have to ask her.

A couple days after the bedtime episode she asked me again after dinner as I loaded the dishwasher. "Do you love me?" she said.

"Of course," I replied, shooing one of the dogs from the dish rack. They both liked to "preclean" whatever we left behind.

"That's what you said last time," she said, handing me the next rinsed plate.

Because of my preparations, I was ready for this. "It happens to be true. My love for you is like a reflex, like breathing, something you just have to do, always there, even when you're not thinking about it."

"Are you saying you don't think about me?" I frowned down at the row of dirty dishes and nudged the dog away a little harder than necessary. My wife is not a lawyer, but she could play one on TV.

"That's not what I'm saying at all. I think about you all the time."

"What is it that you think about me?" Beth shut off the faucet and snapped the dishtowel over the sink before hanging it across the rack on the counter. The other dog immediately tugged it free and ran with it to his bed.

"This sounds like a quiz," I said. I shut the dishwasher door and hit the start button. It whirred into life.

"Maybe it is," she replied. "Maybe it is."

That next Monday in class I lingered purposefully behind, hovering at Señora Nuborgen's desk, pretending to make sure I had everything I needed in my stack of books. The movie continued to run behind me. She hadn't bothered to turn it off, sitting silently at her desk as the post-bell rush blew past her. She seemed to be staring down at her hands in her lap. I cleared my throat.

"What can I do for you, Josh?" she said without looking up.

"Last week . . ." I've always been at a loss for words, not able to find the right ones without significant planning and preparation. Even with the weekend to ponder everything she'd been saying to me, I still couldn't figure out what to say.

"Yes?" Her eyes were red-rimmed, like she'd been crying.

"Last week when I said, *estas en amor* instead of *estoy en amor*, you said that was true, that you weren't in love . . ."

"Yes?"

"Well, what I was wondering is, what about Señor Nuborgen?"

"What about Señor Nuborgen?" Her eyes sparkled. I wondered if I was being teased.

"Don't you love him?"

"Señor Nuborgen," she said, "is a very nice, thoroughly boring man who was eminently available, and given the current situation, I'm infinitely grateful that I met him."

"What current situation?"

"I'm not talking about that," she said.

Not knowing what to say, I lapsed into Spanish, maybe hoping that whatever came out was nonsense. "Esta guapo?"

"No, Señor Nuborgen is not handsome, but then I'm not particularly *bonita*, am I?"

I shrugged. She wasn't. What teacher was? But I wasn't going to say so.

"No," she said. "I'm no Jennifer Mecklenberg. I guess I never was, but there was a time when I wasn't so bad, if you can believe that."

I remember trying to really look at her, at who she might've been, but all I saw was what we saw in just about every teacher. Someone old. Someone tired, someone weary. They were like a different species. To us they all looked beaten, defeated, bags under the eyes, living on endless cups of break-room coffee, dragging themselves toward the summer break when they could recharge at least a little, and Señora Nuborgen was no different, though she'd declined more than most over the year.

I tried to look her in the eye. "I can," I said. Just then the film ran out; the end slapped against the uptake reel. Señora Nuborgen came out from behind her desk and went to the projector. "You're a sweet boy, Josh. Jennifer Mecklenberg would be lucky to have you, particularly compared to that braying ass Andrew Collins." Switching off the projector, she quickly threaded the end back through the sprocket on the original reel and switched the machine to reverse.

"You know," she continued, "she and Andrew are having problems."

"Huh?"

"I heard her crying about it to one of her friends in the bathroom. Seems like he's been stepping out on her at college."

"Stepping out?"

"He's having sex with other girls."

It took me a moment to digest the implications of this, the multiple meanings. Andrew Collins and Jennifer Mecklenberg were having problems. Andrew Collins was having sex with other girls. *Other* girls. Jennifer Mecklenberg had had sex. With Andrew Collins.

"Don't look so surprised," Señora Nuborgen said. "Lots of you are having sex."

I suppose this was true, but I was not among them, and during class periods as I gazed one row over and two seats ahead at Jennifer Mecklenberg's lovely legs, at the small bones of her wrist, and I imagined gaining the privilege of touching her in those places, my thoughts about her never turned to actual sex. Kissing, of course, maybe a hand on the outside of her cheerleading sweater (maybe even inside), but sex? Ridiculous. Jennifer Mecklenberg was not someone you had sex with. Unless you were Andrew Collins, apparently.

Señora Nuborgen placed a hand on her hip and cocked her head at me. "Not you, though. That seems clear enough." The movie finished rewinding, and Señora Nuborgen snapped the projector off. She came toward me and rested a hand on my cheek. There was a faint wisp of rubbing alcohol at her wrist.

"We're running out of time, son," she said.

I have been looking for these love looks on the faces of my students, but I do not see them there. Maybe it's because I teach college instead of high school and these kids are already skilled at masking these things from the likes of me, or maybe my influency at expressing love makes me equally poor at reading it in others.

It's strange even to think of them being in love, *real* love, because they do seem like children to me, especially now that I've realized I'm old enough, biologically anyway, to be their fathers. Of course, some of them must be in *real* love, since they're about the age I was when I met Beth. Maybe it's different for them because these kids do not date; they "hang out" until "hanging out" turns into a relationship. If you ask them, these are their stories. *We were just hanging out and then one day we hooked up.*

In our time there was no "hanging out." There was predator and prey, pursuer and pursued, and while sometimes women were the pursuers and men the pursued, it was usually the traditional way around. Beth likes to tell people how I was dating someone else at the time I started pursuing her, which is shamefully enough true, though I haven't felt any shame over it in a long time. It depends on her mood how she tells it. One version is meant as flattery, a confirmation of our shared destiny together. The other is offered as evidence of my theoretical inconstancy, a floating of the possibility that because I've jumped ship once, I may do it again. She has quizzed me about this other girl, asking me if I loved her.

"Apparently not."

"Why do you say that?"

"Because I dumped her for you."

"That doesn't speak so well of your character, does it?" She usually smiles when she says this, but I know this Beth. This is the Beth that asks me if I love her.

Señora Nuborgen was right, we were running out of time, so the next day I no longer pretended I had a reason for staying behind to talk to her. "Looking for a woman's advice, eh, Josh?" she said. She had all the drawers of her desk open and was removing each object, one at a time, conducting a brief inspection before placing some in a cardboard box and throwing away others.

Señora Nuborgen laughed. She held up one of those troll dolls that you stick on the end of a pencil and then twirl to make the hair stand on end. She handed it to me. On the back someone had written "Señora N." in permanent marker. "Who did this?" I said.

"I don't remember. It was a long time ago." I handed it back to her. She held it over the box briefly before tossing it into the trash.

"What should I do?" I said.

Señora Nuborgen paused in her sorting. "I'm going to betray my feminist sisters here, Josh, but I'm going to tell you a simple truth. Women like passion. They like romance, and above all they want you to be passionate about *them*. You are quite literally sick with love, my young friend, so we know you don't lack the passion. The question is if you can express it. Do you think you could tell her how you feel?"

"Definitely not."

"Well, can you show her then?"

"What do you mean?"

"If you can't tell her that you love her, you should show her, make a demonstration of your love. A gesture, a grand gesture."

"Like what?"

Señora Nuborgen fished a stack of index cards out of the desk and dumped them in the cardboard box. "When I was your age, I pooled my graduation money and went to Spain for three weeks, Andalusia . . . Málaga, the southern coast."

None of these things meant anything to me. She may as well have been speaking of Mars.

"I stayed with a host family and spent my days and nights just wandering the city. My Spanish at the time was no better than yours is now, so I kept to myself, soaking it in, dreaming of the day I could come back and understand it all. It's when I decided to major in Spanish. I figured I'd teach during the year and spend my summers in Spain." Señora Nuborgen took a bundle of pencils bound together with a rubber band and placed them in the box. "I was pretty dumb. I've never been back."

"Why not?"

"I teach high-school Spanish, Josh. Do you know how much they pay me? Do you think it's summer-home-in-Spain money?"

"Right. But maybe someday . . ."

"No, not someday, Josh," she said.

"OK."

"Anyway," she said, "there was a boy with a scooter. I saw him on the street outside my host family's home the fourth or fifth day. He had the most beautiful long, dark hair, dark eyes, brown skin. It was the festival month, and no one save the street vendors did any work.

They've got the right ideas there, Josh. He wore a short-sleeve button-up shirt that he let flap open in the breeze. He would wait outside for me, holding a helmet under the crook of his arm, and once he saw me make eye contact he'd pat his hand on the scooter seat."

"What did you do?"

"I ignored him. I was seventeen. He must have been at least twenty. I was a virgin!"

I must have blushed.

"That's right, an innocent young girl being pursued by a swarthy foreigner. Scandal!" She swept her arm blindly into the recesses of the desk, reaching for any straggling objects before continuing. "I even tried changing up my schedule of comings and goings, but he was always there, smiling, patient, patting the seat. I began to dream about him, not always good dreams, like him driving his scooter to the bottom of the Mediterranean Sea with me on it. But finally, on my last day, my host mother was sweeping the stoop out front and she saw the boy gesturing to me and I asked who he was and she said, *Él es inofensivo,* he is harmless, and so I went over to the boy and put the helmet on and climbed onto the scooter."

She was enjoying her own story. I imagine now that it was something she'd never told anyone before, but she'd been rehearsing it in her head for quite some time, waiting for the right moment. "And what happened?" I said.

"We rode. In a day we saw everything it had taken me better than two weeks to experience on foot. It was the same, but faster, a blur. I hugged him tight around the middle and quickly learned to lean into the corners. My Spanish vocabulary was terrible, his English worse, so whenever he said something while smiling I laughed, and whenever his face was straight I nodded seriously. Eventually, as we made a final turn and I realized we were heading for home, I felt deeply sad. Sometimes endings are new beginnings, but this just felt like an ending. I remember leaning my head into his back, pressing my whole self against him. I remember his smell, but I couldn't describe it to you. It is deeper in me than that. As we got closer to the host family home he drove more and more slowly, so slowly we practically tipped over. Back in front of the house, I got off the scooter and faced him as I removed the helmet. My hair was sweat-matted to my face. He took the helmet and swept the hair from my cheeks and pressed his hands to both sides of my face and he tilted my head up and pulled me toward him. I closed my eyes. I had been kissed before, badly, but I was certain this time was going to be different, and I was right."

She looked at me, and for a moment I thought I could see that girl again, transformed by her own story. She appeared lost for a moment, gazing down at the box holding the keepsakes from her desk. She hefted it briefly before dumping everything from it into the garbage. She continued.

"He pressed his lips to my forehead, and even against my flushed skin they felt warm, but even so, I shivered in his arms. He tilted me back and looked me in the eyes before releasing me, and in an instant he was back on the scooter and gone, leaving me there wobbling in the street. He never said it, Josh, *Te quiero*, but I felt it."

As I've made clear, my Spanish was not so good, but I knew that word, *quiero*. "But that means *I want you*, not *I love you*," I said.

"Very good, Josh," she said. "Exactly."

When I talk to my students about writing stories, I speak of the importance of showing and telling and how they are inextricably linked, dependent on each other. This is why when my wife asks me if I love her and I say, "of course," it is not always enough. Sometimes, but not always. It is all tell and no show. I know she would like me to show her, but I'm not sure how, worried that any expression I risk will seem inauthentic. I am simply bad at romance, but not for lack of wanting to try.

Just before Beth and I were married, we had to meet with our officiating minister and declare our intentions. Neither of us were or are churchgoers, so we picked her out of the Yellow Pages, the first one who agreed to marry two people she'd never met, provided we were acquaintances and not strangers to her by the time of the ceremony. I don't remember her name, Reverend something, though I guess I could look it up on the marriage license, but she was a big woman, tall, and she seemed oversized for her small rectory office. She was kind, making small talk before turning to me and asking what she said was the only question that really mattered, "Why do you wish to marry this woman?"

I told her of Beth's best traits, her beauty, her kindness, our shared values, the sense that we belonged together, all true things, but nonetheless a pretty lackluster answer. I even knew it at the time, but the Reverend smiled and nodded at each new thing that came out of my mouth. I spoke for what seemed like forever, I guess hoping that quantity would substitute for quality.

Once I finally petered out, I smiled wanly at the Reverend, then at Beth, and the Reverend turned to Beth and said, "And why do you wish to marry this man?"

Beth reached over and took my hand and looked at me while speaking to the Reverend and said, "Because when he tells me he loves me, I believe him."

The next day was the last day of school, and all pretense of classroom decorum was discarded completely. The final installment of *Don Quixote* played, but the chattering never stopped. Girls sat on their boyfriends' laps. The kid next to me whose name I cannot conjure for the life of me slowly ripped each page out of his textbook and made paper airplanes that he sailed randomly around the room. Señora Nuborgen was at her desk, blocked by the projector screen in front of her. We were all pent up, ready to explode, and I suppose Señora Nuborgen realized that any effort to contain us was pointless. When Quixote died, disillusioned and alone, some wag went, "Awwwww, that sucks, dude." The resulting laughter outstripped the actual humor. Everybody but me leaked out of the room before the final bell even rang.

I switched off the projector as I made my way to the front. Señora Nuborgen was busy stacking the books from her shelves into boxes.

"Why are you packing up everything?" I asked.

"I'm not going to be back next year, Josh," she replied.

"Why not?"

She paused with her back still to me, reaching for the highest shelf with her fingertips. "Can you get these for me?" she said.

I came around the desk and began handing her the books one by one. "Where are you going?" I said.

I handed her three more books before she spoke. "I'm moving on, Josh."

"Don't you like it here?"

She paused again. Her chin quivered and I looked away. "I love it here."

"Then why not stay?" I asked.

I silently passed down more books until she wiped her arm across her eyes and said, "So have you figured out what you're going to do?"

I had, sort of. There would be an end-of-year party at someone's house whose parents believed it was safer to let the kids drink under some adult supervision. I'd never gone to any of these, but I'd go to this one, and once there I'd figure out how to show Jennifer Mecklenberg I loved her.

"Good," Señora Nuborgen said. "It's important to remember that whatever happens, it's the right thing."

"What do you mean?"

"Trust me, Josh," she said. "I know what I'm talking about. The worst thing is to wonder."

I handed her the last book, and she dropped it in the box without looking. Then she reached up and placed her hands on my cheeks and pulled my forehead down to her lips and kissed me there. Her lips were dry and cracked against my skin. "Good luck, Josh," she said. When I looked at her again, she was crying.

I also talk to my students about the necessity of suspense in their stories, of the need for tension, even for surprise that is built in, that is organic to the story, unexpected, yet also right.

But I will spare you any attempt to build suspense over what happened at the party. There is nothing to show. There were no surprises. Jennifer Mecklenberg was there, Andrew Collins was not, the seemingly perfect scenario. But if she was Saturn, her friends were her rings, while I was some kind of moon in a very distant orbit. I hugged the perimeter of the party, circling for a chance to get closer, hoping I would do the right thing when the time came. She had signed my yearbook that last week, "You're awesome!!!!!! Let's hang out this summer xoxo, Jennifer." I took it as encouragement even as I knew that Jennifer Mecklenberg's name was in a lot of yearbooks and that "awesome" was probably her most frequently used word.

At one point during the party she saw me and waved with the tips of her fingers, and I tilted my warm cup of beer back in salute. Even from a distance her eyes looked glazed over from the alcohol, and who even knows if she knew who she was waving to. It soon became apparent to me that if this was the time, it was not the place, or vice versa. At some point, while playing a drinking game, she sprinted from the room to go vomit in the bushes. I don't think I stopped loving her then, but I at least stopped wondering about whether or not it was possible for me to show her this. The chance that Jennifer Mecklenberg might also love me seemed vanishingly small.

Later that summer, just a few days before I was to leave for college, I sat at the breakfast table, shoveling cereal into my mouth, and my mother handed me an open page of our tabloid-format local weekly. It was turned to the obituaries. "Wasn't she one of yours?" she said, tapping the page.

The heading just said "Nuborgen" in bold type. The text said that Sylvia Nuborgen, longtime teacher at Greenbrook High School, had passed away the previous week after a several-month battle with ovarian cancer. She was survived by her husband, Jameson P. Nuborgen, and her parents, Theodore and Beverly Portnoy. The couple had no children. Donations to the American Cancer Society were requested in lieu of flowers. The service was to be held the day after I was scheduled to leave for school.

When I looked up, I could not see my mother for the tears in my eyes.

Is that surprising? I don't know. At the time, I should've seen it coming, but I didn't.

And so, because I am not capable of telling Beth how I love her and why I love her, I will have to show her. I will show her by writing a story. I will show her by writing these stories.

ACKNOWLEDGMENTS

This book is dedicated to my teachers, of which there are too many to name them all, but special thanks to Philip Graham, Robert Olen Butler, and John Wood. Thanks as well to friends and colleagues from whom I've had the pleasure to learn much along the way, including, but not limited to Nick Johnson, John Griswold, and Marlene Preston.

Thanks to Michael Griffith for his brilliant editorial touch, Susan Murray for her careful copyediting that saved me from more than one embarrassment, Michelle Neustrom for the elegant design, and to Rand Dotson and Lee Sioles at LSU Press for shepherding the book into the world. It takes a village.

College of Charleston has been good enough to provide a secure place from which to do my work, and I'm grateful for the kindness and care of my colleagues.

The title and one of the book's epigraphs belong to my friend Mark Brookstein, lead singer and drummer for Chicago's legendary band The Rolls. I've borrowed them without permission, but he'll understand.

As always, this would be impossible without the support of my loved ones: the families Warner and Sennello.

Finally, thanks and love to Kathy. My love *is* like a reflex.